THE IMMACULATE

THE
IMMACULATE

FIRST CINEVISTA EDITION

Kevin Alyn Elders

Cinevista

Screen Novel Series ™

Seattle & Villefranche Sur Mer

2018

Cinevista, Inc
A Screen Novel ™

Copyright © 2018 Cinevista, Inc.
THE IMMACULATE
Kevin Alyn Elders

ISBN-13: 978-1-943673-04-9
ISBN-10: 1-943673-04-7

A disclaimer: THE IMMACULATE is a work of fiction. Names, characters, places and incidents are products of the author's imagination or are used fictitiously, and are not to be construed as real, except where noted. Any resemblance to actual events, locales, organizations, or persons, living or deceased, is entirely coincidental, except where noted.

The Cataloging-in-Publication Data is on file at the Library of Congress

Contents

ACKNOWLEDGEMENTS

Surprisingly, this is the first work of fiction I've written that has frightened its buyers. I've sold dozens of screenplays during my three decades in the movie business, *The Immaculate*, in its screenplay form, was no exception. Yet even after having bought it, two Hollywood studios didn't have the courage to make it. A narrative that might be equally compelling for both Christians and Muslims was probably too far afield from their comfort zones. Regardless, their decision led to the writing of this novel. I want to acknowledge all of you who pushed me to do it. You know who you are and I am thankful God blessed me by putting you in my path—your love for this story has kept its flame burning.

As always, to you, the reader, I am immensely grateful for your time and I hope you'll enjoy the journey.

Easter Sunday, 2018
The Pacific Northwest

For my mother,
Who nurtured me
Who endured me
Who gave me my first
glimpse of the Immaculate

Prologue

1978 was one of the first years Detroit resumed making destroyer class luxury cars after the oil crisis, the Mercury Grand Marquis being one of its largest. Opulence abounded, especially the rear leather seating which the young boy luxuriated in while his parents in front fought to stay awake by listening to the radio.

They'd been driving all night. Ever since his younger sister died the now family of three drowned their sorrow in road trips hoping somehow new destinations would erase old memories. For the boy, those memories were painfully fresh. He eyed the empty seat next to him, the one that until a year ago was always occupied by his sister. The Leukemia ravaged her quickly, her youth withering in months, her last breath wheezing out in seconds. The boy would never forget that. He would always struggle to understand how life worked. How a six-year-old girl could suffer. How an innocent could lose her rightful place on the planet while others less innocent continued to hold onto to theirs. Still, he had his mother's love. And as she turned back to check on him, offering her warm, adoring smile, he felt safe.

Until he wasn't. The harsh oncoming headlights sliced through the interior of the car abruptly. His mother turned startled, blinded by the glare. She realized, all too late, that her husband had been dozing. Her scream got lost in the devastating roar of six tons of metal colliding together. The boy's seat belt held him. It saved him from the impact of the front seat jackhammering backwards to within an inch of his chest as the Mercury and the oncoming vehicle pancaked together at sixty miles an hour.

He didn't know how long he'd been unconscious. Perhaps it was the smell of gas that awakened him. Perhaps it was the smoke. The vehicles were only slightly ablaze at that point. It was hard to see anything as he struggled to free himself from the gnarled cage that enveloped him. The rear window was shattered. As he made his way towards it, he saw his mother's hair oozing with blood, her face unrecognizable. His father was crushed flat and motionless, pinned behind the steering wheel. The boy began screaming. There wasn't really a point to it. No one could hear him as the front of the car exploded sucking all sound and oxygen from a thirty-foot radius around it. Kicking, screaming, the boy managed to pull himself out of the Mercury to the asphalt. That's when he saw him. The driver of the other car. The model of it was impossible to make out as it had accordioned into a fiery ball of smoldering metal. But the driver, the man crawling towards him, was clearly visible. The man was covered in blood. It had soaked the white collar of his black cleric's garment and was oozing down the silver crucifix dangling on the priest's chest. The priest called out to the boy asking if he was okay. The boy stopped screaming. Paralyzed for an instant, the boy's eyes fixated on the bloody crucifix, his rage boiling inside. Snapping, the boy lunged violently at the man who killed his parents. He scratched and ripped at the face of the helpless priest, who, startled and terrified, tried to subdue the boy's frenzy.

The police finally arrived. It was only then that the officers managed to separate the child from the priest. The boy just slumped to the pavement. Catatonic, his eyes stared somnambulant at the crucifix which had fallen to the ground and was ablaze in the river of gas streaming from the fuel tanks of the Marquis.

Chapter I

Forty years later, in the skies above Bannack, Montana, a lone crop duster cut its way through ink black cumulus.

On the isolated prairie below, six heavily armed men in menacing balaclavas swarmed a towering wooden rural church preparing for an unfathomable siege. They took up sniper positions behind cars in the crowded parking lot while their leader, tall, devout and indomitable, focused his jade-colored eyes on the massive wooden doors protecting the church's entrance.

Inside the stark Victorian structure, nearly every pew was empty as its congregation had crowded together in front of the altar. At least one hundred parishioners locked arms and were compressed into a circular human wall as if to protect someone from the impending onslaught. Father Haines, the parish's defiant, bible-clutching priest, motioned his flock closer together while exhorting from scripture.

"... Do not fear, I will strengthen you for I am your God and I will uphold you with my

righteous hand!" Haines bellowed.

The terrified congregation started singing a desperate chorus of "*Mighty to Save and Keep*" clutching their children and watching their protectors, four shotgun-toting parishioners, who stood guard at the church's front doors.

The men at the doors nervously monitored the enemy outside in the parking lot. They frantically used their cellphones to communicate with the FBI assault force rapidly assembling on a tarmac twenty miles away.

THE NORMALLY SLEEPY airport in rural Montana was covered with a horde of government Suburbans responding to Bannack's first-ever terrorist attack. The joint FBI/SWAT assault team urgently loaded its gear into choppers as a Lear 60 landed on the tarmac.

Frank Larson, the restless FBI agent in charge, headed to the Lear as its turbines wound down and its ramp dropped to the tarmac.

Secret Service Agent Sol Turner was the first one out of the Lear. As he hurried down the ramp towards Larson, it was clear he'd changed a lot in the forty years since he was trapped in the back seat of the Mercury. The boy had grown into a fearless forty-five-year-old sentinel, a soldier, a protector of last resorts. Numbed and hardened by his memories, Turner's focus reigned supreme. Cellphone to his ear, Sol raised a finger to Larson signaling that he was wrapping up an urgent conversation.

"—he'll be fine, Anne. Michael will be *fine*," Sol continued firmly into his cellphone. "We just *have* to trust the experts."

Two thousand miles away, inside St. Jude's Hospital in New York, Anne Turner, an attractive woman buried in panic, disagreed. She nervously followed a boy strapped to a gurney as ER techs wheeled him into intensive care. She was on her cellphone with Sol, her now estranged husband.

"There are no *experts*, Sol!" Anne responded, trying not to come unglued. "You know damn well Dr. Jergens has never seen this disease!"

Sol was moving double time now with Larson alongside him. He eyed the chopper and assault team waiting impatiently for him on the tarmac. The job demanded a dispassionate fealty and, as hard as it was, he knew he had to wrap up the call.

"Jergens is the best man they got down there," he told his wife desperate to reassure her. "He's in good hands."

Inside St Jude's, Anne watched frantically as

the doors to intensive care slid shut after her son's gurney disappeared inside.

"Michael's terrified, Sol!" she pleaded into her cell. "Dammit, you should be here with your son!"

On the tarmac, Sol's heart was inside that hospital but his body had to steel itself for battle. "I would if I could, Anne. Dammit, you *know* that! Look, I'll check in—but I *have* to do this. I'm sorry." He hung up with a military discipline. He cauterized his pain stoically, he'd become an expert ever since the police pulled him away from his parent's burning wreckage. Unfortunately, Anne didn't have the same training. Her eyes teared as she stared through the small windows of the ER doors while a frenzied swarm of nurses and doctors administered to her son.

On the Montana tarmac, Sol finally got his status update from Larson as they headed to the choppers. "Best estimate we have is a ten man terrorist assault force," Larson informed him.

"Any IDs on the combatants?" Sol asked.

"Everyone's betting homegrown," Larson answered. "FBI hasn't logged any foreign chatter."

Sol shook his head. "Don't buy it. NSA disagrees. Sheikh Ansari's cell has been texting about this boy for weeks. Are we sure the kid's even in there?"

"Hundred per cent," said Larson. "The local pastor confirmed it."

They finally reached the choppers. As their turbines wound up for takeoff, Larson eyed Turner warily.

"Look, Turner, I'm not bucking chain of command here, never would, you know that's not how I roll. But how the hell did Secret Service get jurisdiction on this?"

"The President called at 3 a.m., Frank." Sol answered with a reluctant smile. "When he does, I get on planes."

Sol signaled the pilot as he climbed inside the chopper and yelled over the roar of the turbines, "Let's get airborne!"

Rotors revved as Larson followed Turner inside. Sol strapped himself in eyeing the empty sky above them that, for now, was clear and pristine as the choppers surged upwards.

IN STARK CONTRAST, thirty miles away above the besieged church in Bannack, massive dark clouds were coalescing, as if the heavens frowned upon the terrorists taking up battle positions in the church's parking lot beneath them.

The jade-eyed Muslim leader studied the

brewing storm above him. He lifted a gray megaphone to his lips and turned towards the church.

"You must all understand that we don't wish to harm you!" scratched out of the megaphone as Jade Eyes yelled into it. "We only want the boy!"

Inside the church, the parishioners still huddled in terror as Jade Eyes' voice continued to boom in from outside.

"Release him to us and we will spare you!" they heard Jade Eyes promise.

Sister Agnes, an elderly nun, approached Father Haines at the altar, her eyes pleading.

"Father, perhaps … perhaps if we talk to them. If we could just—"

"They will not negotiate!" Haines barked, cutting her off. "They are here for only one thing—something we cannot give."

"No," she responded defiantly. "We *can* give them our truth. There are babies in here. We have to try, we have nothing to lose!"

Stubbornly, Sister Agnes headed to the front door. Before the armed parishioners could stop her, she slipped outside brazenly onto the front steps of the church.

She stopped abruptly, seeing assault rifles aimed at her body. She eyed them fearlessly.

"We have no fight with you!" she yelled.

Jade Eyes motioned his men to lower their weapons.

"Turn over the boy and we will leave," he warned her. "Defy us and the suffering begins."

Sister Agnes watched four of his men move large barrels of what was presumably gasoline towards the perimeter of the church.

Behind the church's front doors, one of the armed parishioners spotted the barrels outside.

"They're going to burn us out!" he bellowed to the congregation.

Outside, Sister Agnes began walking towards Jade Eyes, her eyes steadfast, her reprimands streaming, "There are young children inside! Some of them newborn, their whole lives ahead of them! Surely, your God would not allow you to—"

"*STEP BACK*!" Jade Eyes warned her icily.

But Agnes didn't stop. She continued to walk towards him. Jade Eyes grew agitated as suddenly one of the armed parishioners poked his shotgun out the church's front door and fired, killing one of the terrorists. An unfortunate development. One that triggered every remaining terrorist to return fire. Their assault rifles blazed, shredding the church doors.

Sister Agnes was caught in the crossfire. She

took four lethal rounds to the chest. She slumped feebly to the pavement, slaughtered in the exchange. Jade Eyes moved towards her waving angrily at his men.

"Burn it! All of it! *BURN IT DOWN!*"

His men started pouring naphthalene all over the exterior wooden walls of the church.

Behind the front doors, the armed parishioners returned fire. Father Haines looked on helplessly as more armed parishioners broke hundred-year-old stained glass windows to fire at the parking lot. The noise echoed violently. Children screamed terrified.

A MILE AWAY, the response team's choppers sliced through the sky. Sol watched the church in the distance and the surreal, dark cloud formation coalescing above it.

Outside, in the church's parking lot, the battle was raging. The armed parishioners behind the massive barricaded doors kept their assailants at bay.

Jade Eyes' men finished pouring the naphthalene around the perimeter of the church. He signaled them to ignite it.

The blaze erupted violently. Jade eyes waited for it to take as suddenly, miraculously, thunder roared and the clouds above them burst.

A tempest of rain and hail poured down from the heavens. The wet, icy avalanche prevented the flames from building. Jade eyes stared at the skies above him incredulous.

Inside the church, the parishioners watched the rain pounding the parking lot in awe. Father Haines rallied the huddled crowd.

"And though a mighty army surrounds me, I am not afraid for your rod and staff will comfort me ...," Haines preached, reading from the open Bible in his hand.

The congregation began singing again, anemic at first, clinging to their faith as the gunfire built outside.

In the parking lot, the terrorists were no longer firing at the church. Instead, their weapons were raised and firing on the choppers. Sol's cavalry knifed through the rain, descending from the clouds with a Valkyrie-like lethality.

The choppers swooped down and landed in the distance. A fearless swarm of FBI and SWAT team members streamed towards the church's parking lot, firing on the run, pinning down the terrorists with an unrelenting wail of lead.

Jade Eyes crouched behind a bus as a hail of bullets pelted his surroundings. He yelled at his men to fight on as, inside the church, the armed parishioners battled on bravely seeing the SWAT team approaching.

As the gunfight raged, Larson's team unleashed a furious barrage as Sol raced towards the eye of the storm. He homed in on Jade Eyes, who was dodging bullets as he ran menacingly towards the church's doors.

The SWAT team's counter assault was merciless. In seconds, more than six assailants fell dead to the pavement.

But inside the church, the situation was bleak. Jade Eyes and three of his men had managed to breach a side barricade. They unloaded on the armed parishioners and three other women who had come to their aid. Seven parishioners were slaughtered in as many seconds. A terrified crowd started screaming as the barricaded front doors burst open.

Sol and four members of his team rushed down the aisle quickly killing two terrorists with headshots while engaging the remaining gunmen on the run.

In desperation, Jade Eyes grabbed a small girl from the crowd. He pulled her backwards towards the altar as the last member of his cell was killed by another headshot just inches away from him.

Larson's remaining team stormed the church

from the rear doors as Sol drew down on Jade Eyes who kept his gun mercilessly at the girl's head.

Sol eyed Jade Eyes venomously. "It's over. All your men are dead!"

Jade eyes stood there defiantly, his gun pressing harder against the girl's forehead. She wept uncontrollably, terrified in his grasp. Jade Eyes turned towards the parishioners who huddled in fear just yards away from him. He eyed them sadly, almost compassionately, desperate to warn them, "The boy ... his fate ... this is on your heads. Don't you see it? You will only bring him death."

With that, he whipped the gun from the girl's head, and before Sol could fire, Jade Eyes stuck the gun in his own mouth and blew out the back of his head.

Jade Eyes dropped to the floor beneath the large crucifix hanging above the altar as the girl ran back to her mother. Sol made his way down the center aisle of the church as the crowd huddled in front of the altar finally began to part.

The parishioners stared horrified at the dead as they separated and slowly revealed the precious cargo they had been shielding.

As the last of the trembling bodies peeled away, Sol eyed the congregation's treasure— a seventeen-year-old boy who stood alone in front of the altar. His features were youthful with an ageless, pale olive skin and haunting hazel eyes that stared at the slain beneath him with an unsettling calm.

Sol made his way towards the boy.

"Aadam Samuel James?" Sol asked him unceremoniously.

The boy looked up at Sol finding an odd comfort in his presence.

"Yes," he answered quietly.

"I need you to come with me," Sol said as he motioned the boy towards him.

Father Haines pushed through the crowd unsettled, "He's with us! Why on earth would you—"

"Because you're all at risk if he stays."

Haines continued defiantly. "Look, you *don't* understand. This child is—"

"—a citizen of the United States and subject to its laws," Sol answered preemptively.

Haines started to protest, but the boy intervened. "It is all right, Father," Aadam told Haines calmly. "I shall go with them. They mean me no harm."

With that, Aadam walked away from the altar, past Haines, past Sol, past the dead who the boy eyed painfully as the stained glass windows above him bathed him in a surreal, multicolored light.

As Larson's team escorted the boy outside, Sol finally looked up to the sky realizing the clouds had cleared and the rain had stopped.

Chapter II

The helicopters arrived back on the tarmac at Bannack. As Sol and Larson escorted Aadam off the chopper and headed towards the Lear, a herd of reporters and television crews choked their path to cover the story. Sol signaled his team to keep them at bay. Sol and Aadam climbed up the ramp into the Lear as its turbines wound up readying for takeoff. All cameras zoomed in on Aadam's young face as he disappeared inside. The footage would be broadcast live on televisions everywhere, the fodder for a media frenzy set to captivate the world.

A BLACK CHEVY SUBURBAN was parked beneath a modest apartment building in Washington, D.C. Inside the Suburban, a news station on its radio blared—

"... Christians across America held a midnight vigil last night after a federal assault team rescued Aadam Samuel James, the boy who many believe is—"

A hand tapped the radio's *off* button abruptly

cutting off the announcer. The hand belonged to Sol. It moved back to the steering wheel wearily. He'd been up all night. He stared at the windows of the apartment building looming above him, waiting for something.

He zeroed in on a light that just went on inside an apartment on the fifth floor. He pulled the keys from the ignition and climbed out of his government SUV.

AT THE DOOR to the fifth floor apartment, Sol pressed the doorbell repeatedly. Its ring wasn't loud but its piercing staccato rhythm orchestrated by Sol was certainly enough to unnerve anyone inside. Anne Turner finally opened the door. Disheveled and still in her bathrobe, she clearly wasn't a fan of his technique. Irritated, she let him into the apartment.

"You could have called."

"Didn't want to wake you," Sol said as he surveyed the overly furnished apartment like a man who was rarely exposed to it. "How is he? I tried Jergens twice at the hospital."

"The operation lasted two hours. The prognosis isn't good."

Sol frowned. That wasn't the answer he wanted. "Well, we've got to give it time."

"Time's his scarcest commodity," she responded contemptuously. This was one of her ex-husband's qualities that irked her more than any other—his dogged optimism in the face of personal adversity—his unwillingness to face a seemingly inevitable tragedy.

"C'mon, Anne, it's a new disease. Cures come out of nowhere." Sol's brain refused to go to the place where Anne had wallowed in for the past two weeks. "I'm not writing off Michael's chances just because some board certified neurologist gave him six months to live."

"There you go again. As usual, in your mind, *you* get to decide. Sorry, but I don't share your optimism."

"Well, our marriage might not be on life support if you did."

"Is that all it was?" she said, moving to within an inch of his face. "Then quit the job and move back in. Spend his last few months holding him in your arms."

Sol looked at her a long time, as if somehow trying to reconcile his own frustration before answering. "You know I can't do that," he finally said quietly.

"Yeah. So much for optimism," she said dryly as she moved away from him and into the kitchen. "I'm going to the hospital. Are you coming?"

"Soon. I have to get down to—

"—sure you do," she said, cutting him off. "What was it *this* time?"

"You didn't see the news?"

Anne shook her head, irritated. The fact he would think she'd be watching television while pulling an all-nighter in the ER praying their son would survive should come as no surprise to her but it stung all the same.

Sol continued, oblivious. "There was a terrorist attack. Church in Bannack, Montana."

"Bannack? That's a one-horse town. Drove through it on my way to Bozeman when I was a kid," she said surprised. "Why a church there? What were they after?"

Sol eyed her cynically. "Well, according to the adoption papers, just a seventeen-year-old orphan from Bannack. But according to the evangelicals—the son of God."

INSIDE AN FBI holding facility in a twelve story building on the outskirts of Washington, four armed officers waved Sol and Larson through a metal detector. As they reclaimed their guns, keys and badges, Sol probed Larson getting himself ready for the upcoming interrogation. "Is the kid awake?"

"Don't think he slept," answered Larson.

"Does the press know where we're holding him?"

"Not yet."

"Good. We don't need a bunch of bible thumpers screwing up the investigation."

"So, I take it you're not a *believer*?" Larson chided.

Sol smiled as they reached a metal door guarded by two Secret Service agents. He turned to Larson. "I need a favor, Frank."

"Name it."

"There's a Doctor Jergens at St. Jude's who just operated on my son. Can you have someone patch him through? He's been difficult to reach."

"Sure, I'll make it happen." Larson assured.

Sol thanked him with a confident nod. The two of them went back a long time. Working together hadn't always been easy, but it had been predictable. They'd put their lives in each other's hands at times. And since they were both standing there, it seemed to have worked out.

The agents unlocked the metal door. Sol walked inside and headed to a spartan but brightly lit holding room surrounded on one side by a mirrored wall where superiors were presumably watching from behind.

The object of their attention was the boy seated in the only chair alongside a barren table—Aadam Samuel James. Father Haines paced behind him. Both looked up as Sol entered unceremoniously.

"Morning, gentlemen. I trust we've been accommodating?" Sol said with a forced smile.

"Hardly," Father Haines responded angrily. "I've asked for our attorney."

"Really? And why do you need an attorney?" Sol said amused. "You haven't been charged with any crime."

"Because you are treating us like prisoners!" Haines answered, pointing to Aadam. "You people do not understand what you're dealing with!"

Sol locked eyes with Haines a moment to make sure his response was measured, not out of respect for Haines but in deference to the unknown onlookers behind the mirror. "I don't mean to burst your bubble, *Father*, but I've been an atheist since my parents were murdered when I was five. So if you don't mind stepping outside—"

"I *stay*," Haines said defiantly. "I am his *legal* guardian."

Sol opened the door to the holding room. "The white collar won't stop me from dragging you out," Sol said icily. "So if I were you, Father, I'd reconsider."

Haines eyed Aadam who nodded calmly for him to leave. Haines headed reluctantly to the door. "May the lord forgive your insolence," Haines muttered passing Sol.

Sol ignored him. He shut the door and turned to Aadam. The boy studied Sol, unafraid of confronting his interrogator's eyes.

"You're not an atheist," Aadam said quietly.

"Excuse me?

"Your parents weren't murdered, it was an accident. You blame God for lack of intervention but not lack of existence"

Sol studied him, thrown. "Who have you been talking to?" he demanded.

"No one," Aadam responded. "Ask Mr. Larson. I've been locked in this room."

Sol decided to move on. He opened a file and buried himself in its contents, ignoring the memories the boy had stirred up inside him. He started reading from the file with a military precision and a numbed, clinical detachment. "Your adopted name is Aadam Samuel James. Orphaned. Parents unknown. Left on the steps of the rectory in Father Haines's parish. Your body was badly bruised. Doctors say you were beaten. Do you have any recollection of that?

Devoid of any emotion, Aadam answered promptly, "I have no memory of anything before my time spent with Father Haines."

"And the so called *miracles*?" Sol asked cynically. "Do you have any memory of those?"

"The essence of existence is miraculous. My interaction with this essence can hardly be called a miracle."

Sol closed the file impatiently. The kid's unwavering calm was getting to him. "Do you believe you're the Son of God, Aadam?"

"We are all children of God," Aadam said, looking into Sol's eyes.

Sol smiled, biting his lower lip. Playtime was over. "Look, let's cut the bullshit," Sol said as he leaned down into the kid's face. "You can be their Christ or their Satan, doesn't matter to me. They want to drink the Kool Aid, I'll supply the cups—all I wanna know is why *ten Muslim extremists* came to *kill you*?"

"Their intention was not to harm me."

"Quit screwing around, Aadam! People are *dead*!" Sol threw black and white photos of the presumed Muslim extremists on the table beneath Aadam as he pressed the kid angrily. "Abu Nazeer, Tariq Massoud, Ali Mukdir ... *Do you know these people*?!"

The kid just shook his head as Sol studied

him frustrated.

Sol turned suddenly hearing someone enter the room at an irritated clip. It was Simon Novak, the Director of National Intelligence. Mid-fifties, insanely fit with a linebacker's-chest, Novak was supremely pissed. "Turner, step outside," he told Sol forcefully, accentuated with the curt wave of his finger.

Sol was taken off guard but he dutifully complied as Novak motioned to a bald, sharp-featured man wearing a black turtleneck. The bald man headed inside towards Aadam accompanied by an unsettled Father Haines. They crossed Sol's path as he followed Novak outside the holding room.

Larson eyed Sol confused as Novak corralled them both in the corridor. Rattled, Sol eyed Novak firmly, "Sir, who'd you just let into my interrogation?"

"Arthur Burke. The Agency's top psychiatrist," Novak answered, with a hint of his own frustration. "It's a formal handover. He'll be taking custody of the boy."

Sol eyed Novak confused. "I thought the President assigned—"

"—He assigned you to protect him, not offend him or trample his civil rights."

Sol studied Novak. He could see Novak's

heart wasn't in it, that he was just following orders and Sol would make it his business to find out who issued them. Sol stared at his boss. "Sir, we've been through a lot together and I don't buy for one second that you think this kid is holy."

"Doesn't matter what I think, Sol," Novak responded. "It matters what the President thinks. And right now he wants to meet the kid and he wants him treated warm and fuzzy till he does."

The metal doors to the main holding room door opened. Haines, Burke and Aadam filed out. Novak signaled the Secret Service agents to escort them out of the building. As they walked past, Aadam turned briefly to Sol and told him quietly, "You should call your son."

The agents led Aadam away, leaving Sol unsettled and confused behind them.

A HEAVILY BANDAGED twelve-year-old boy was tethered to his gurney by his life support lines inside the recovery room in St. Jude's. Michael Turner was barely conscious but he could feel his mother softly stroking his forehead as she sat there alongside him. She fumbled for her cellphone as it rang hoping its upbeat and strangely out of place Bachian ringtone wouldn't disturb her son. She answered quietly. "Hello?"

Sol was frustrated by bumper-to-bumper traffic driving in his Suburban on the Washington beltway. "I'll be there soon, two hours tops," he assured her. "How is he?"

"Better," Anne answered. "But twenty minutes ago his heart rate spiked out of nowhere and he stopped breathing."

Sol stiffened. That would have been exactly the time when Aadam told him to call. Sol brushed off the coincidence. Normally, an atheist's faith was grounded in provable fact. Sol's was grounded in anger. And the fact his son was struggling to survive, possibly yet another unbearable tragedy in Sol's future, was stoking that anger. But he kept it contained to help his wife remain calm.

"I spoke to Jergens. He said sometimes that happens. Something to do with the drug. But he assured me it would only be temporary. Can you put Michael on?"

"He can't talk," Anne replied curtly, almost irritated he asked.

"I know, but put him on. Just put the phone to his ear," Sol pressed.

Anne obliged begrudgingly. She softly put her smart phone next to her son's ear. The boy didn't stir as Sol began speaking.

"Michael, I know you're in a lot of pain. And

I know you're wondering why I'm not there. I'll be down as soon as I can. You're going to be fine, I promise, Champ. Your dad's gonna make it happen." Sol sounded brave and convincing, the effort as much for himself as for Michael.

His son just laid there half-comatose as Anne pulled the phone back to her ear. "I can't tell if he hears anything. Where can I call you if he gets worse?"

Sol eyed the turnoff to Andrews Air Force Base a quarter mile ahead.

"Camp David," he told her.

Chapter III

A MILITARY CHOPPER landed on the Camp David tarmac under heavy military guard. Its passengers unloaded. Sol, Aadam, Haines and Burke were herded away in black Suburbans.

Inside Camp David's stately but rustic living room, Raymond Sykes, the National Security Advisor, conferred with a restless silver-haired man who was serving his third year in his second term as America's President.

"... the Saudis are nervous," Sykes told his Commander-in-Chief. "The boy's an obvious challenge to their supremacy."

"That's why a Muslim designate needs to round out the inquiry," the President told Sykes. Sykes responded with an *I'm on it* nod.

The President turned expectantly hearing a knock on the door.

An aide poked his head in, "They're here."

"Show them in," the President commanded with a smile filled with anticipation.

Sol was the first to enter followed by Arthur

Burke. The President greeted him warmly.

"First off, Sol, I want to thank you. Excellent job in Montana." The President rose to shake Sol's hand.

"Just wish I'd gotten there sooner, Sir," Sol said humbly.

"Justice isn't always punctual nor is it pretty. But the important thing is that it gets served." The President turned to Burke. "So, Arthur? You've had twelve hours with him, what's your opinion?"

"His motor and memory skills are normal. No signs of trauma. Healthy appetite, even healthier ego," Burke answered dryly. "Whatever the kid's selling, Sir, he's certainly a believer."

"But you're not convinced?"

"I'm biased. I'm an agnostic. The chances are one in a trillion."

The President smiled while picking up a bible on his desk. "That's what they said the first time, Arthur." He turned back to Sol. "So where is he? I'm anxious to meet him."

Sol signaled the aide who opened the door, motioning to someone outside. Aadam finally entered, followed by Father Haines. The President approached the boy with a hopeful reverence.

"I'm John McCormick," the President told Aadam warmly, extending his hand.

Aadam smiled politely as he shook the President's hand. "I know who you are, Sir. It's an honor to meet you."

"The honor's all mine, I assure you." The President indicated the sofa while nodding to Haines and Aadam. "Please make yourselves comfortable. Can I get you anything?"

"We're fine, Sir. Thank you," Haines answered as he and Aadam took their places on the sofa. Aadam eyed Sol briefly feeling that Sol was watching him. He was. It was more than occupational habit. Sol was trying to get a handle on the kid. His instinctive take on someone would have usually kicked in by then but in this regard, Aadam had eluded him.

The President didn't take his eyes off the boy as he began the signature folksy chatting style that was the hallmark of the thirty-year politician's commencement of an interrogation. "Sol tells me you don't think the men came to harm you?"

"Absolutely not," Aadam answered respectfully.

"Then what do you think was their purpose?" the President asked.

"To follow their hearts. Their intentions

33

were pure."

"So you're saying they killed with pure intentions?"

"The path to transcendence is littered with the bodies of the innocent," Aadam replied firmly. "And so it will be in Herat. "

The President and Sykes both stared at Aadam a beat and then eyed each other unsettled. Sol watched confused as suddenly a cream-colored phone rang on the President's desk.

"Excuse me for a moment, will you?" said the President. He headed to his desk and answered the ringing phone.

"Yes ... Of course, put him on ... Yes? ..." The President got the news he'd been waiting for from a military commander in the field. But the news wasn't what he expected. His heart sank. "How many?" he said grimly. "... My God," he responded after hearing the answer. "... All right, issue a statement ... No. Don't stonewall it. Tell them the truth. ... Yes, you heard me—the *truth*." The President hung up. He regained his composure and turned to his guests.

"Everything okay, sir?" Sol asked carefully.

The President ignored him and eyed Aadam directly. "There's some people who would like to spend some time with you, Aadam. Would you be opposed to that?"

Aadam answered without hesitation. "If I can serve in this way, I am willing,"

"Fine," said the President. "I'll make the arrangements. I'm assigning you a security detail. For your own safety, of course."

"As you wish," Aadam responded.

Aadam rose, as did Haines, sensing the meeting was over. They said their goodbyes and Burke followed them out. As Sol started to leave, the President motioned him to stay. Sol waited for the doors to close behind the others before he finally spoke. "What was all that about, Sir?"

The President eyed Sol gravely as he responded, "Ten minutes before you arrived, I authorized a Predator strike on an Afghan terrorist camp—village of *Herat*." The President indicated Sykes as he continued, "Now Raymond and I were the only ones who knew. Forty civilians died in that strike. Twelve of them children."

Sykes was reeling. "So the boy knew ..."

"Yes," the President nodded. "But that simply isn't possible unless—"

Sol knew where this was going. His mind headed there after the coincidence in the hospital, Aadam *knowing* when he should call Michael, but no, he wouldn't allow his mind to take that trip then nor would he allow the President. "Sir?" he interrupted. "With all due respect, there *has* to be some other explanation?"

The President eyed him firmly. "Really, Sol? Open your eyes, more importantly, open your heart. Clouds darkened out of *nowhere* above that church and raindrops *the size of walnuts* put out those flames in Montana. That boy has performed a host of other miracles—"

"All scientifically unsubstantiated. All potentially *refutable*," Sol said stubbornly. Sol was revealing his deep inner prejudice and doing so a bit too irreverently for Sykes' taste. The President didn't seem to mind. He was a man comfortable in his own skin, certainly comfortable in his own religion.

"I won't debate the supremacy of science over theology with you, Sol," the President said as he sat down behind his desk. "The boy will be subjected to rigorous examination by a council of experts. And you, my friend, will lead the team that protects him."

Sol hated where this was going. "Sir, perhaps he'd be better served by a believer—"

"Nonsense, you're the best I've got. The fact I'm sitting here after an assassination attempt proves it. And I kind of like the idea of a member from the opposition babysitting the participants," the President said with a wink. Then he eyed Sol firmly, "You guard that boy as you would me, Turner. If any harm comes to him under our watch, the consequences would be absolutely catastrophic."

Sol took a long, reluctant beat before he finally nodded.

Chapter IV

Lahore was the armpit of Pakistan, home to terrorist insurgent groups seeking refuge and a *NO GO* zone for the battle-weary and sometimes terrorist-complicit Pakistani military.

Inside an unkempt apartment above Lahore's bustling downtown marketplace, a young Muslim man, head and face shaved, was fully dressed but asleep on a cot in an otherwise empty room. He awakened with a start. He rolled off the bed quickly and swept the room with the 9mm he grabbed from under his pillow searching for the source of the footsteps.

A red-haired Caucasian appeared in his doorway. Seeing him, the Muslim man lowered his gun irritated.

"You should have knocked. I could have killed you," said the young Muslim.

The red-haired man motioned the Muslim man to be silent. He placed a duffel bag on the bed and pulled out the disassembled Remington M24 SWS sniper rifle inside it.

Then the red-haired man opened a leather folio. He spread out a passport, airline tickets and an itinerary which the Muslim man studied intently. By the time the Muslim man looked up, the red-haired man was gone.

UNDER BEAUTIFULLY VAULTED corridors snaking through the Vatican's administrative offices in the Apostolic Palace, a cleric clothed in black made his way towards a large wooden door at the end of the garish hallway.

Reaching the door, Father Grimaldi stopped briefly to compose himself before knocking. He fiddled with his glasses. They were still new to him, his vision suffering only during the last two months since he turned 50. Still, he was young in Vatican years and it always gave him pause when he was summoned by his elderly superiors. Falling out of favor with Cardinal Amato, the Vatican Secretary of State, the man he was about to have a meeting with, almost always led to *appointments* in far off places. Places where violence and unsanitary conditions reigned supreme. Places Grimaldi hoped to avoid, God willing. Yet if God *willed*, Father Grimaldi would certainly comply since he was, first and foremost, a God fearing man. He valued morality and truth on earth above all else because he feared valuing anything less would lead to hell's eternity. Still, as he knocked on Cardinal Amato's door, he was hoping to find favor inside. His spirits lifted when Cardinal Amato called for him to enter in an uncharacteristically upbeat voice.

Once inside, Grimaldi found Amato rising to greet him from behind his conspicuously ornate baroque desk. Cardinal Amato was slight and diminutive, typical of a fifth generation Venetian, but his Georgetown education and the fifteen years he spent as the Vatican emissary to the United States imbued in him a sense of grandiosity. Amato was somehow bigger than life. His forceful, sometimes overbearing ways overshadowed his requisite Catholic piety. Amato was feared by everyone at the Vatican, some would say feared even by the Pope, but Amato was all smiles that morning and he endeavored to make Grimaldi feel welcome as he motioned for the cleric to sit.

"Father Grimaldi, it's always a pleasure to see you," Amato effused, "and the spectacles are a welcome addition, they make you seem more studious. Though you're hardly lacking in that regard. I've been hearing great things about your work with the Council of Saints."

"Doing my absolute best, Eminence," Grimaldi replied humbly. "Our work is challenging in times such as these. As you know, science's exaggerated revulsion of theism these days has raised the threshold for proof to new heights. A postulator's challenge is daunting."

"But such worldly challenges pale when confronted with the power of our Lord?" Amato chided.

"Most certainly, Eminence. I wasn't meaning to imply—"

Amato dismissed Grimaldi's apologetic response with a smile and the wave of a hand. Amato was anxious to move on to the business ahead of them. He grabbed a closed file on his desk and set it down it front of Father Grimaldi.

"I'm appointing you as head postulator for a very important determination," Amato informed dryly.

"Someone already on our list of designates?" Grimaldi asked.

"No," Amato answered flatly, knowing this would spark a swirl of confusion inside Grimaldi's obsessively methodical brain. For postulators like Grimaldi, who were charged with authenticating miracles as a precursor for the possibility of sainthood, there were standardized lists. Vatican officials would meet yearly to designate possible candidates. Grimaldi's team would be notified and an investigator, a *postulator* in Vatican parlance, would be assigned. The designate list was short and Grimaldi could recite it by heart. The fact he was being appointed as postulator for someone who was not on that list was highly unusual. In fact, in his 30 years of service to the Vatican, he'd never seen it happen. Grimaldi tried to temper his uneasiness as he sought further details from Amato, "Have there been miracles, Eminence? Or just acts of supreme sacrifice?"

"Both," replied Amato. "Go ahead. You may open it." Amato motioned to the file.

"I see," said Grimaldi as he began to open the file, "in what year did the designate pass away?"

"He has not passed," replied Amato. "He is *living*."

"*Living*?!" answered Grimaldi, with a crackle of shock in his voice. With the file open, Grimaldi studied the top sheet he found inside—along with the black and white photo of Aadam Samuel James.

AN ORTHODOX RABBI rocked back and forth, as he prayed at the crowded wailing wall in Jerusalem. The noise of a massive excavation project in the distance overwhelmed the rabbi's pious silence along with the IDF soldier who interrupted him from behind. The two talked briefly shouting to be heard over the din. The rabbi left with the soldier. Both had a newfound sense of urgency.

AN ISRAELI NEWS broadcast was playing on the screen above the desk of a young secretary as the IDF Soldier escorted the rabbi into the office of the Israeli prime minister. As the rabbi walked by, he eyed the images on TV of angry Palestinians rushing a police line as the voice on the newscast blared, "... protests have turned violent as Arabs fight to halt Israel's excavation project near the historic Al-Aqsa mosque. IDF soldiers have surrounded the crowd as tensions flare once again inside the Old City ..." The images seemed to weigh heavily on the rabbi as the soldier opened the door to the prime minister's office. He motioned the rabbi inside.

A world-weary Israeli prime minister looked up from the file on her desk as the rabbi entered her office. She seemed in her late 40s but her short time in office was clearly taking its toll. Israel's elderly political pillars were inevitably falling and giving way to Israel's youth. She was among them but she wasn't foolish enough to discard her reverence for her country's history—for the men who had risked their lives fighting to keep it free. For men who had tracked down adversaries and killed out of necessity—men like Haim Rossen, the powerfully built *rabbi* in front of her. She motioned Rossen to sit as the IDF soldier left her office, shutting the door behind him.

"Thank you for coming, Rabbi Rossen," the prime minister said respectfully. "But in this office would you mind terribly if I called you Haim?"

"You are the prime minister. You out rank me. You may call me what you wish," Rossen answered cynically.

"Good," she said relieved. The tech sector was her background before entering politics. She was still out of her element with former IDF Special Forces soldiers turned Intelligence officers like Rossen. "I'm offering you an assignment, Haim."

Rossen dismissed her with his cold, scorpion-like eyes, "As you no doubt noticed by the way I dress and certainly from the entries in my dossier, I have long since retired from Shin Bet."

"Respectfully, Mr. Rossen, *no one* retires

from Shin Bet and, as you aptly pointed out, I *out rank* you. But if it will make you feel better we are all keenly aware that you've forsaken the gun for the Talmud."

"The Talmud is mightier than the gun," replied Rossen, measured but defiant.

"Then help us protect it because it is about to come under siege."

"I don't understand."

"You will in time," she warned as she slid a file folder in front of the rabbi. Rossen opened it and stared at the picture of Aadam inside.

UNPARALLELED OPULENCE WAS the hallmark of the Royal Saudi Palace in Riyadh. In a secluded, heavily guarded conference room on the ground floor, Saudi heads of state convened with urgency. The Saudi king was in attendance and he looked up impatiently as a bearded Sunni Imam was escorted in.

The cleric was breathless and embarrassed. The cleric bowed in front of the king. The king motioned him closer. There was some quiet discussion between them in Arabic that left the cleric visibly confused. The king summoned one of his aides to hand the cleric yet another file folder. The bearded Sunni cleric opened it and eyed the dossier and photo of Aadam Samuel

James. He studied it apprehensively as a palace servant cleared empty glasses from a table alongside the Sunni cleric. The servant seemed keenly interested in the file.

The servant quickly wove his way with the tray of glasses towards the palace kitchen.

Inside the kitchen, the servant scanned the faces of several workers before he finally locked eyes with a face of a worker that was staring back at him. The worker was the young Muslim with the shaved face and head who was briefed by the red-haired man in Lahore. The servant covertly passed the young Muslim man a folded piece of paper.

The young Muslim moved outside into a corridor to read it. Its contents seemed to fill him with a sense of urgency. He stealthily slipped into the shadows and made his way out of the palace. His bags had already been checked on the Airbus 360 that was readying for its flight across the Atlantic. He had to make sure he was onboard in time to accompany them.

Chapter V

Sol loathed hospitals. He watched his young sister die in one and when they tried to revive his parents after the crash, he had wept for hours outside the ER after that endeavor tragically failed. Perhaps that's why he was ambivalent about being there for Michael's surgery. Perhaps he wouldn't have been brave enough and that would have chipped away at Anne's all too fragile bravery as they waited for the verdict. All this weighed heavily on him as he lingered outside the door to his son's recovery room in St. Jude's. Anne was inside sitting in a chair next to Michael's bed. She looked up as Sol finally came into the room.

Michael could barely move but his face brightened seeing his father. Sol leaned over him, kissed his son on the forehead and presented a forced but optimistic smile. "How they treating you, Champ?"

Michael tried to talk. He couldn't. The drugs were numbing the pain but they just intensified his weakness. All Michael could manage was a feeble squeeze on his dad's finger. Sol hid his overwhelming sadness with an even bigger smile.

"I'm getting you out of here," he assured him. "Box seats at the Red Socks opener. Just you and me. You up for that?"

Michael's eyes visibly teared. Sol fought to keep from crumbling. He turned away for a second to hide the water welling up in his own eyes. That's when he saw Dr. Jergens making his rounds outside in the corridor. "I'll be right back," Sol mumbled as he left the room to intercept him.

Dr. Jergens was somewhat of a legend at St. Jude's. A surgeon and a peer reviewed researcher, he was impeccably refined and inspired confidence in staff and patients alike. But Sol wasn't interested in refinement or scholarly achievements. He was only interested in saving his son. Jergens looked up from a clipboard seeing Sol approach. He tried to get out a friendly greeting. Sol's first words made him realize that wasn't going to be necessary.

"He looks like shit," Sol told Jergens.

Sol was agitated for obvious reasons and deep down he was scared. Jergens knew this but he also knew Sol was a realist, so he didn't pull any punches.

"Michael looks exceptional under the circumstances. Two days ago, we gave him a ten percent chance of survival. The procedure increased it to thirty."

Sol's face dropped. "I need better numbers, Doc. Whatever it takes, I'll get it for you."

"Sorry," Jergens responded, "but we're in uncharted territory with this—"

"That's not good enough!" Sol said angrily. "Dammit, Doc, last month he was batting .400 in little league. Now he looks like he's fifty!"

The staff at the nursing station was glued to the confrontation but Jergens politely absorbed the salvo.

"It's going to take more than bullets and bravado to kill this disease, Mr. Turner. And I promise you I am doing absolutely everything I can. But if you'd like to relieve me of my duties here, now's the time to say it."

Sol stood there a beat. Then finally shook his head. "Sorry. It's just that, it's just ... that boy is all I have."

Jergens eyed him compassionately. "Then let me get back to the work of saving him."

Sol nodded. Jergens put a reassuring hand on Sol's shoulder, then left to continue his rounds.

Anne came up to Sol from behind. She

watched him a moment as he struggled to contain his frustration before he finally turned to her. "How's the optimism now?" were the only four words she could muster.

FOOTSTEPS ECHOED LOUDLY in the neon-lit high security D.C. holding facility as Sol and Larson made their way towards Aadam's holding room. Sol was still shaken from seeing his son and Larson was throwing every bit of breaking FBI intel at him to try and keep Sol's mind off it.

"... CIA and Pakistani ISI both confirm that all the Montana assailants were *definitely* linked to Ansari."

"Well, let's get the formal *Go* to laze that fundamentalist shit and send a hellfire onto his prayer rug," Sol responded.

"Be glad to," said Larson. "But first we gotta find him."

They reached the metal doors outside Aadam's holding room. A Secret Service agent opened them. Larson and Sol went inside.

Inside the outer holding area, Arthur Burke was already sorting three large piles of what looked to be identical documents on a conference table as Sol entered with Larson.

"How's he holding up?" Sol asked Burke. He

was still uncomfortable with Burke's presence but he was resigned to it.

"The boy's calm. Composed" Burke answered.

"Smooth operator."

"Or the real thing."

Sol eyed Burke cynically. "Thought you Freudians were skeptics?"

"Well, faced with indisputable evidence of the impossible—" Burke said as he eyed the documents on the conference table, "—let's just say it gives one pause."

The interchange was interrupted as three more men were ushered inside by Secret Service agents—Father Grimaldi from the Vatican, Rabbi Rossen from Tel Aviv and Hassan Nassif, the Muslim cleric from the Royal Palace in Riyadh.

Sol had been briefed on who they were and the fact they were coming to be part of the make-shift *inquiry* he'd be leading, but *Rabbi* Rossen was the only one of the three he knew personally. He nodded to him with a slight hint of disdain.

"How are ya, Haim?" Sol asked Rossen. "How's it feel to enter the country legally this time?"

There was a palpable tension between the

two men. This caught Burke off guard.

"I take it you two have met?" Burke asked Turner.

Sol never took his eyes off Rossen. "Oh, yeah. We go *way* back. Don't we, *Rabbi*?"

Rossen, ever stoic and impatient, didn't dignify the question with an answer. Sol wasn't really waiting for one. Instead, he handed each of the three men one of the identical folders Burke had been preparing.

"I assume the three of you know each other's backgrounds. The files contain everything you need to know about the subject of this inquiry. You'll find the kid inside." Sol motioned the three men towards the inner holding room. Sol followed them inside accompanied by Burke.

Aadam was sitting calmly behind a table with Father Haines pacing restlessly behind him as the men finally entered. Sol forced an upbeat greeting to Aadam and Haines.

"Morning. It's a bit chilly in here. Want me to turn up the heat?"

"We're fine. How is your son, Mr. Turner?" Haines asked.

Sol ignored him. He just wanted to get it over with. He waited for everyone to be seated around the table next to Aadam then laid out the ground rules for the matter at hand.

"The session will last eight hours," Sol said turning to Aadam. "These men have all reviewed detailed reports of your background and the documentary evidence of the so-called—*divine actions*." Sol could barely get the phrase out but he soldiered on. "Copies of the supporting documentation are in these files. Mr. James you are not under oath here but the President, all of us actually, would appreciate it if you answered truthfully."

"The truth may not always be comprehensible to you," Aadam answered politely, "but when I answer, the truth is what it shall be."

Sol eyed the kid a beat. For the moment, Aadam seemed unflappable. Sol had an instinct that was about to change. "Great!" Sol finally answered, forcing a smile. "Let's get this done."

THREE HOURS LATER, the interior of the holding room seemed like a furnace. Aadam's interrogators had been at it fast and furious, perhaps the questions heated up the molecules in the air. When trying to authenticate divine actions or *miracles,* as a layperson would refer to them, one had to be incredibly precise, skeptical and perhaps even lethal. Various religions over the centuries had killed millions in their defense, relying on the authority of divine inspiration and seeking the validation of divine action. Sol didn't buy any of it, of course, but he did enjoy seeing Father Haines squirm when trying to describe an incident in Aadam's past, the time when he first laid eyes on Aadam as a child.

"... Sister Agnes could not make out the driver of the vehicle that dropped him off," Haines told the group while Nassif and Rossen studied Aadam as if he were a Da Vinci forgery. "The driver left Aadam on the steps of the rectory. It was the dead of winter. He was shaking from the cold. When Sister Agnes spotted him, she rushed outside to bring him in. Aadam could not have been more than nine or ten at the time. We'll never know for sure. He carried no documentation. And from that day forward, no one from his past, the driver who dropped him off or otherwise, ever came to claim him."

Nassif, the Muslim Cleric, pressed Haines skeptically. "And will we be allowed to interview this *Sister Agnes*?"

Sol answered for Haines, "Unfortunately, she was gunned down outside the church in Bannack by your brethren."

"Terrorists who take lives are not my *brethren*, Mr. Turner," Nassif bristled. Sol didn't care. He just wanted to get this behind him. He eyed his watch impatiently.

WHEN SOL EYED his watch a second time, it was two hours later and they were still at it.

Haines was describing Aadam's upbringing at the Bannack orphanage. How the other orphans looked up to him. How he comforted and mentored them. How, as a young teen, he began preaching at the church.

"… Aadam's calling came early to him. I'd say he was fourteen when he first told me he would like to become a priest. He had a manner that made the other children feel secure. An ability to inspire," Haines recounted fondly. "The congregation began to believe in him. Especially in light of the miracles."

Rossen looked up from the documents he'd been studying. "*Miracles* where *you* always seemed to be present. Correct, Father?"

"I was his legal guardian, he was under my care. Of course I would be present," Haines responded irritated.

Rossen turned to Aadam. "Did any *miracles* take place without his supervision?

"What are you inferring?!" Haines blurted out, glaring at Rossen.

"That perhaps you facilitated—"

"The occurrences you refer to were manifestations of divine grace. They can manifest in you as they did me," Aadam interrupted, his lack of timidity irritating Rossen.

Rossen flipped through pages of Aadam's file. "Sorry Mr. James, but I've never cured an epileptic nor made rain fall from an empty sky.

"Perhaps you haven't tried?" Aadam said calmly.

Sol smiled seeing Rossen back off. He turned relieved to see Larson come in with bags of lunch from a fast food restaurant nearby.

"Let's take a break for a minute shall we, gentlemen?"

TWENTY MILES AWAY inside the downstairs baggage claim at Dulles Airport, the clean shaven Muslim man who was so eager to get out of the Royal Palace in Riyadh had finally arrived in Washington. He grabbed his luggage and seemed overly careful to steer clear of any TSA security circling the crowd of arriving passengers. He headed to passport control. When he got in front of the customs officer, he presented his passport. Oddly, it was American. A fake, but a U.S. passport all the same. And obviously good enough to circumvent U.S. border security software. The Muslim man left customs without incident. In moments, he hailed a cab which whisked him away from the crowded airport.

SOL NURSED HIS fifth cup of coffee. He was jittery from the caffeine but he listened intently to the current *miracle* that Haines was recounting.

"... The pickup truck sped around the corner. I don't know if the driver was drunk, reckless or both but he must've been driving at least twenty miles an hour around that turn. A six-year-old boy under our care was crossing the intersection at the time. He didn't have a chance. Had he ran, it might have been worse," Haines recounted tragically. "As it was, he was struck by the truck's left bumper. It knocked him flat to the pavement. The truck's front tire ran over him as the driver swerved to avoid him. I'd imagine he never knew what happened to the child. The driver never stopped. He accelerated away and disappeared before we could even see his plates. Aadam was outside the orphanage at the time. He witnessed the whole tragedy. He was the first one to reach the child. The child's body was mangled. Lord knows how many of his bones were crushed and shattered. When the paramedics arrived, they were a witness to the child's injuries. He was motionless, hemorrhaging badly internally. He wasn't breathing. While they were preparing the gurney to take him to the hospital, we all watched as Aadam leaned over him. He ran his hands tenderly across the boy's injuries and stayed with him inside the ambulance. As you can read in the file, when he got to the hospital, the child had almost fully recovered. It was miraculous! The paramedics didn't know what to make of it."

Father Grimaldi was grappling with the implications of this as he reread the documentation of the incident contained in the file. If true, this was the type of divine action that, to the Catholics at least, was incontrovertible. But *if true* was the operative phrase.

"I see the police noted the truck driver was never apprehended," Grimaldi said to Haines. "And I also see the attending paramedic who first arrived on the scene is now deceased. Besides your recounting of the facts, there is not much more to substantiate the child's—"

"Father Grimaldi, you have the paramedic's full report of the child's extensive injuries that he signed at the time," Burke said jumping in. "And if you'd read further you'd see you have the admitting doctor's report. It clearly states the child's flesh was bruised with internal bleeding indicated *but* the MRI he was given after arriving at the emergency room validated he had healed. No broken bones, no fractures. Certainly no sign of being hit by a truck at twenty miles an hour."

"An incident that was only witnessed by a dead paramedic and members of his congregation," Nassif interjected skeptically.

"And a flock determined to validate their savior, no doubt?" suggested Rossen, piling on.

Father Haines bristled. "I'm giving you the facts. Lab reports don't lie. The paramedic gave his statement. Aadam healed the boy. A boy who would have been dead on arrival without his laying on of hands!"

"All right, we got it, Father. We got it," Sol said impatiently. "Can we just move on to the next one? The rest of you can weigh in on everything when we're finished here. That is, if we ever finish. Which may take a miracle of its own. So save one up for me, will you, kid?" Sol added as he winked to Aadam sarcastically.

Aadam stared back at him, nodding slightly as if to say—*Yes, your miracle is coming*. Normally, Sol would have found humor in that but there was something in Aadam's muted but sincere response that unnerved him, shook him to his core.

NO OTHER MIRACLE was as compelling as the one Father Haines recounted two hours later. Nassif, Rossen and Grimaldi were immersed in the documentation of the event. It involved a tragic fire. One that raged in a nursing home in downtown Bannack two years earlier. It started in the kitchen igniting a propane tank that blew a massive ball of flame through the security doors and into the ward housing seventy-five frail seniors. As Haines described it, Sol watched Aadam. The boy seemed visibly distraught from the memory of it.

"Aadam and I were ministering to the disabled when the fire broke out," Haines recounted. "The ward was sealed off from everyone else. I still don't know why. The orderlies couldn't reach us. The sprinkler systems above us finally came to life. The sprinklers soaked us from above subduing the fire around us. We managed to help everyone leave by forcing the rear door open. The residents ran outside. It was then that we heard the screaming. It was from the rear ward, the ward reserved for the infirm. The sprinklers had failed to turn on there and the ward was consumed by flames. I admit the screams terrified me. I was frozen from the horror of it. And then it happened."

"Then *what* happened?" Sol asked impatiently.

"Aadam raced towards those flames. I tried

to stop him. He was just wearing a sweater, nothing to shield himself, but he went inside that raging inferno anyway. The screaming continued as the flames grew bigger. We thought for sure everyone inside that ward, including Aadam, would be killed, burned beyond recognition. And then he emerged—dragging two of the infirm alongside him, swatting out the flames on their clothing. But no flames, no flames whatsoever were on Aadam. He was completely unscathed! We took the two residents he had saved from his arms expecting Aadam to go outside with us to safety but he went back! He said there were two more inside, so once more he braved the flames, emerging minutes later with the last two residents trapped in that ward. Again, the clothing of the residents was burned, charred, smoking but not Aadam. He was unaffected by the flames, saved by his selfless, fearless act. Yet again, it was miraculous."

"Of all the incidences of divine action here today, this one I can corroborate" Father Grimaldi said solemnly to everyone's surprise."

"Really? How so?" Sol said skeptically.

"Unbeknownst to me at the time, a colleague of mine was dispatched by the Church to investigate," Grimaldi informed the group as he handed Sol a document he fished from his brief-case. "I brought along his report. Over ten witnesses saw Aadam emerge from that fire unharmed. In this case, the evidence seems incontrovertible."

All eyes shifted to Aadam. Burke, Nassif, Grimaldi, all of their skepticism was starting to soften. Everyone except for Rossen—and Sol, of course, who checked his watch for the hundredth and last time.

"Sorry, gentlemen but we've gone well past our scheduled session time," Sol told them as he bundled up his files on the table. "I'm sure our distinguished panel has plenty to digest."

"Should anyone require further documentation, my office is at your disposal," Burke said rising.

Exhausted, the postulators all stood and gathered their respective paperwork. Aadam was the only one who remained seated. He was studying Rossen. Rossen finally caught on to this returning Aadam's gaze unintimidated.

"God forgives those who forgive themselves," Aadam said to Rossen.

Rossen smirked. "You mistake me for someone with a need to atone."

"The faces that haunt you have found their peace," Aadam continued. "They know nothing of their murder."

Rossen suddenly lunged at the boy, grabbing him hard by the neck and yelling at him—"I murdered no one! No one! Understand me!"

Sol jumped in and pulled off Rossen. The rabbi backed off, throwing up his hands as if to say it was over. Sol pointed at Rossen infuriated. "Outside, Haim! *Now*!"

Rossen nodded and left the room. Sol eyed Aadam. Wondered what the hell was going on between them.

Moments later in the corridor, the entire group filed out past Rossen who was leaning against the wall waiting for Sol. Sol was the last one out. He waited a beat for the group to reach the elevator doors down the hall before he privately confronted Rossen.

"That outburst was inexcusable, Haim. And whatever you are, you're certainly *not* someone who lets a kid get under your skin."

"I apologize, Turner," said Rossen quietly. "You're right. That wasn't me. Especially now. I'm just baffled as to how he knew?"

"Children die tragically all the time in Gaza, Haim."

"But the press *never* ran the story. Trust me; we're on top of these things. Not one report. *None*." Rossen responded unnerved.

"So where's it written an omnipotent God relies on reporters?" Sol offered with a wry smile.

Rossen laughed. "Still—perhaps we missed one report. But how would that boy have known?"

"You're a *postulator* now, Rabbi. Mere mortal minds like mine aren't equipped to help you."

The two shared a warm smile. Whatever had transacted between them in the past, agents at cross-purposes, allies operating against each other's interests, all seemed to be relegated to the burial ground of the forgiven.

Their brief moment was interrupted as Burke called out from the elevators. "Are you two coming?"

Sol nodded and he and Rossen headed to the open elevator doors.

A FULL MOON mitigated the winter's normal darkness outside the Federal building that night as two black Suburbans pulled up to the entrance.

Secret Service agents climbed out as Sol exited the building's main doors escorting Haines and Aadam towards one of the waiting government SUVs.

"Where will they take us?" Haines asked Sol

on the way.

"Until we apprehend the people responsible for the attack, you'll both be staying in a safe house. The apartment's secure and it's nice. A lot nicer than mine—"

Before Sol could finish—Thwapp! A bullet pierced Haines' forehead and the back of his head exploded onto the pavement.

Sol spun around as his agents swarmed Aadam desperately trying to see where the shot came from.

On top of a skyscraper opposite the building, the bald, clean-shaven Muslim was reloading the M24 sniper rifle that he received from the red-haired man in Pakistan. He quickly aimed his scope at Sol's entourage across the street but they were hunkered down behind a Suburban. The Muslim man waited for a clean shot.

From behind the SUV, Sol couldn't see the shooter but he knew from the bullet's trajectory that the sniper was up high. He grabbed his radio as Aadam hovered agonized above Haines' dead body.

"Get a chopper over that roof!" Sol screamed into his walkie. He grabbed Aadam and jerked him back towards the second Suburban, both of them rising ever so slightly. Bad move.

Thwapp! The sniper's second bullet whizzed past Sol and blasted into Aadam's back. Aadam went down. Sol jumped on top of him to cover him from any more incoming as he screamed into his radio, "He's been hit! He's been hit! Help me get him inside!"

Twenty stories above them on the roof of the building across the street, the sniper disassembled his weapon. He shoved it into a duffel bag and moved quickly towards an access door on the roof. He spun hearing the roar of a turbine as a police chopper knifed over the roofline. It had overtaken him stealthily, climbing up from below. An approach from above would have given their prey more time to escape. The two SWAT team riflemen hanging out of the chopper had the sniper right where they wanted him—frozen in their spotlight with his hands above his head on the roof.

The chopper moved closer. Then the Muslim sniper made his move. He whipped out a 9mm from his jacket—emptied its 17 round clip as the chopper spun around defensively and the SWAT team riflemen jumped down on the roof under cover. The Muslim fired their way when they reappeared on the other side of the chopper but the hollow points from the sniper's 9mm were no match for the blaze of .30-06 rounds streaming from the SWAT team's semi-auto rifles.

The sniper fell to one knee, hit twice in the abdomen and once in the neck. He tried to stand back up. He shakily fired his last three 9mm rounds. Relentless, the SWAT team unloaded the last forty rounds in their clips riddling the sniper's already mutilated body with their bullets. The sniper kept staggering backwards with every shot until he finally stumbled over the edge of the roof. He fell violently, arms thrashing, twenty stories to the street below.

Sol watched the sniper's body pancake to the pavement with a muted thud. Traffic screeched to a halt as Sol eyed the sniper's shattered, mangled flesh.

He turned back towards Aadam who was on the floor inside the lobby shielded by the other agents. He grabbed his radio, barking, "Alright, we're clear! Repeat: All clear! Get that ambulance in here NOW!"

Chapter VI

Sol found himself inside yet another hospital. This time his mind wasn't on how much he loathed these places. It was on Aadam, his charge, a boy who, whatever his past, didn't deserve a bullet in his torso that might ultimately take his life.

Sol stayed alongside Aadam's gurney as the paramedics raced it towards the ER. Aadam was unconscious on top of it.

Once inside the fully prepped ER, a trauma team quickly went to work on him. The lead surgeon motioned Sol to stay outside. Sol complied and stood guard outside the ER doors with two other agents. The shooter was dead but others might be coming. Sol played the escort exit from the federal building over and over again in his head. He had scanned the rooftops in all directions before letting Haines and Aadam outside. The sniper had to have been concealed at that point. Or maybe he missed it. Either way, Haines was dead and Aadam could be next. Sol was the agent in charge; the blame would fall on his shoulders. Nothing fair about it. It just went with the job.

THE SURGERY LASTED five hours. Aadam still hadn't regained consciousness. He was recuperating in a hospital bed in a private room. Sol was in the room with him while two Secret Service Agents guarded the door outside. Sol was on his cell with Larson. He was deeply troubled by something—the sniper's bullet— the one that hit Aadam in his torso. The surgeons hadn't found it and Sol wanted it.

"… The second bullet has to be near the main doors, near the steps," Sol said emphatically into his cellphone to Larson.

"Nothing. Checked it all, every inch of it." Larson responded into his own cell, still at the scene of the shooting. "We swept the building clean."

"Well, sweep it again," Sol ordered. "It has to be there. It wasn't in the kid's body. What about the sniper?"

"Guy's a ghost. We scrubbed his DNA through every database."

Sol's mind raced. He drank the rest of what would add up to his sixth cup of coffee. "Maybe the guy was a floater with the terrorists at the church? Maybe he was manning perimeter there and we just didn't spot him?"

"Don't buy it," answered Larson. "Those guys were definitely Sheikh Ansari's crew. All post-op chatter backs that up. But no one's staking a claim on our shooter."

Sol started to respond but stopped abruptly sensing something behind him. He spun around and stood there breathlessly. Next to the hospital bed, the *empty* hospital bed, was Aadam. He stood there totally calm, tugging at the IVs in his arms.

"Can you help me take these out?" Aadam asked Sol. "They're annoying and unnecessary."

Sol just hung there a moment, floored. He put his cell back to his ear. "Call you right back." Sol put his cell in his pocket and moved over to Aadam.

"Sorry, I didn't know you were on the phone," Aadam said.

"No, no. No worries. Tell me ... why are you standing? A moment ago you were unconscious in that bed?"

"I don't know. I'm not the one who bestows consciousness but in this case I'm definitely happy to be the recipient of it."

"Ok, whatever," Sol replied, "but just lay back down and keep those IVs attached until I get a doctor in here to check you."

"Call who you wish, but I'll stand from now on." With that, Aadam pulled the remaining IVs from his body. Sol rushed outside to get the attending doctor.

THREE HOURS LATER, Sol paced outside a windowed examination room once again on his cell. Through the glass behind him, he watched a team of doctors examining Aadam.

"... Sir, I saw the MRIs. They took *three* of them just to make sure. There was a minor and I mean *minor* trace of the bullet. You'd never see it if you weren't looking for it. And the surrounding tissue ... it was barely traumatized. It's almost—"

"—Miraculous?" said the President pacing behind his desk in Camp David on the other end of Sol's call.

Sol was conflicted and confused. But he had to face the facts. "Maybe ... I just ... I just don't know," he told the President."

"As an atheist, Turner, you're probably unfamiliar with the saying *it's more important to know God than to know answers*. Those words might be helpful in times such as these."

"As atheists, Sir, we've decided there's nothing to know."

"Well, maybe it's time to revisit that," the President chided. "No matter, the three postulators have submitted their preliminaries."

"And? What's their determination?" Sol asked hesitantly.

"They all remain appropriately skeptical but they're unanimous the miracles are plausible. Absent any scientific explanation, Grimaldi and his Catholic superiors, at least, are prepared to admit that they are divine."

Sol eyed Aadam who was staring back at him through the glass in the examining room. "So what now?" Sol asked the President, still watching Aadam. "They make him a saint?"

"Not sure," replied the President. "That's up to a very old man who's anxious to meet him."

"Who?" Sol queried.

"The Pope," the President answered.

MILES AWAY AT St. Jude's, Anne Turner was sitting next to another patient in a hospital bed. But this one was still tethered to life support. Michael was sleeping peacefully beside her. The audio was turned off but the *breaking news* played on the television. Anne watched live footage of Sol coming out of the other hospital with Aadam, alive and well, standing beside him. Not wanting to wake Michael, she turned up the volume ever so slightly to hear the broadcast.

"... Aadam James appears to be fine after miraculously surviving the second attempt on his life. Believers from all faiths have swarmed the streets ...," a reporter announced on the broadcast as footage cut to a massive crowd assembled outside the hospital. Spellbound, Anne watched her husband who was in the middle of it.

Miles away, on the hospital steps, Sol and his agents struggled to corral Aadam who, messiah-like, moved through the crowd embracing the faithful, all hungry for his touch. Sol finally herded Aadam into a Suburban and it pulled away.

Inside the SUV, Sol and Aadam stared out at the throng. At faces teary-eyed and reverent—faces desperate for hope, passionately waving signs. Sol focused on the largest sign that read—

LORD, PLEASE HELP US
PROTECT YOUR SECOND SON

IT WAS UNUSUALLY late for anyone to be in the Israeli prime minister's office, but the night was historic and tensions were flaring all across the region. The prime minister's secretary was gone but the TV was still on above her desk. Vivid images of violence flashed across its screen. " ... *Hundreds are now dead in Jerusalem, all tragic casualties from the protest that continues to rage over the excavation near the Al-Aqsa mosque,"* the reporter declared breathlessly. Then the broadcast's footage cut to protesters yelling at the cameras with rage in their eyes and fury in their screams.

But across from the secretary's desk, an equally violent protest raged in the prime minister's office. Rabbi Rossen was inside yelling angrily at the prime minister. She held her ground screaming at the infuriated Shin Bet agent at the top of her lungs. The Rabbi was being forced to do something he loathed. Ultimately, he would comply but not before venting his rage. The prime minister endured it. For the sake of Israel, for the sake of the *order* that might otherwise collapse.

SIX THOUSAND MILES away from Jerusalem, Secret Service agents stood guard outside a Washington, D.C. brownstone that was functioning as the temporary safe house for Aadam James.

Inside an upstairs bedroom, the drapes were

drawn and Aadam was kneeling by his bed, writing feverishly in a small, leather-bound book. His hand wrote in ancient script, possibly Aramaic, or some derivative of it, until suddenly, Aadam looked up startled. His body was frozen in shock until he started shaking, convulsing violently. He fell down flat on the floor, writhing uncontrollably.

THE NEXT MORNING, Anne's car was parked with its engine running in the parking lot of Andrews Air Force Base. Anne was in the driver's seat. Sol was alongside her in the passenger's seat. He closed a briefcase on his lap and reached for his carry-on in the back seat. She watched him, the scene all too familiar.

"I'd almost forgotten this life," she mused. "Picking you up and dropping you off at airports—the time alone in between."

"It could have been worse," Sol replied dryly.

"Maybe ..." she said, almost wondering aloud. She turned to him tenderly and grabbed his hand with eyes pleading for comfort. "Will you do something for me?"

"Sure. Name it."

"Ask him to help Michael."

"Oh please, c'mon, don't go there. Don't ask

me to stand in that long line. I'm not buying into any of this."

"And what if he's *real*?"

"Well, then the last few chapters of your bible are pretty clear on that," he answered cynically. "You better stock up on food."

She released his hand and turned away, fighting with herself not to unload on him. He reconsidered seeing how fragile she was.

"Alright, alright. Look, I'll ask him, ok?"

Anne turned gratefully, nodding with a smile to push back her anguish.

Sol spotted two black Suburbans driving up to escort him to the jet waiting on the tarmac. He turned back to Anne.

"Michael will pull through this. He's strong. He's our son. He'll pull through."

Anne nodded, desperate to believe it. Their faces were close. Close enough to kiss. But it had been too long. Sol nodded goodbye and climbed out of the car. She called out after him.

"Remember to pray for him in St. Peter's!" she yelled. "God listens. Even to you!"

Sol smiled, nodded reluctantly and headed to the Suburbans where Aadam watched them from inside through tinted windows. Anne couldn't see him. But she could feel him.

Chapter VII

A white Gulfstream G5 sliced through the sky. Storm clouds coalesced below but at 40,000 feet Sol's entourage was safely above them.

In the rear cabin, Burke was at the starboard window seat engrossed in a journal of psychiatry as Sol came out of the restroom. Sol took a seat next to Aadam who was staring fascinated at the billowy cumulus below.

"Was the view like this on the way down?" Sol asked the boy.

"From where?" Aadam replied.

"Heaven." Sol smiled. Aadam didn't. "Sorry, bad joke," Sol said.

"No, just bad timing."

"Yeah. Why's that?" Sol asked.

Aadam continued to stare out the window. "I lost a father yesterday."

"... Oh, shit ... Sorry again," Sol replied realizing how insensitive he'd been.

"It's okay," Aadam replied. "I'm sure you can relate."

Sol leaned back in his seat, dark memories

instantly transforming his mood.

Aadam finally turned to him. "The drunk driver that killed your parents—he was a priest, yes?"

"Yes," answered Sol with a palpable bitterness.

"Can you forgive him?"

"No," Sol said sharply.

Aadam studied Sol a moment before responding. "Yet you want your son to forgive you?"

"For what?" Sol bristled.

"His pain."

"This disease is new, it's—"

"—Not the disease. The abandonment he felt when you broke the sacred bond of your marriage."

"Marriage isn't *sacred*. It's just what people do when they're vulnerable," Sol replied.

"Is that what it was for you?" Aadam asked.

Sol stared at him a long beat. Finally shook his head. "No. At least not at first." Sol shifted gears. "Look, Aadam … can I ask you something?"

"You're free to ask me anything you wish."

"Okay. Just who the hell are you?"

"Who do you want me to be?" responded Aadam calmly.

"My wife wants you to be the saint who saves our son."

"And I want you to be the saint who forgives the priest," replied the boy.

Sol just stared at him, hanging there, as the jet's turbines roared outside. The G5 was beginning its descent.

ON RUNWAY SIX at Rome Fiumicino Airport, the G5 came in for a landing. Three shiny full size Range Rovers sped towards it. In seconds, carabinieri flowed from inside them forming a well-protected perimeter around the jet. Sol was pleased. Whatever bad things might happen to the kid in the future, it would for damn sure not be happening on his watch.

FORTY MINUTES LATER, the three Range Rover entourage was escorted through the busy streets of Rome by six carabinieri motorcycles weaving past the Coliseum towards the Vatican.

Inside the middle Range Rover, Sol sat in back next to Burke. Aadam soaked it all in, awed by his first glimpse of ancient Roman and Christian monuments, his eyes filled with the innocent wonder of a small child.

Finally reaching the Via DI Porta Angelica

at the edge of the Vatican, the Range Rovers came to a tall, heavily guarded metal gate. Beneath the backdrop of a towering St. Peters Basilica, the gates opened, and the vehicles were waved through by colorfully uniformed Swiss Vatican guards.

AFTER A BRIEF wait in the lobby, a bishop escorted Sol, Burke and Aadam though the garish vaulted corridors of the Apostolic Palace towards the heavy wooden doors at the end of the hall. The bishop didn't bother to knock; presumably, the Secretary of State was expecting them. As they entered, Cardinal Amato was already walking around his desk to meet them.

"Welcome to the Vatican," said Amato smiling warmly.

Sol nodded respectfully. Burke smiled politely. Aadam was too busy taking in Amato's impressively ornate office and the massive grounds outside. Amato approached the boy.

"Aadam, I am Cardinal Amato." The cardinal extended his hand.

"Hello," the boy said, shaking it.

"So what's your impression of our little city?"

"That great sacrifice was required to build it."

Aadam's tone made Amato bristle ever so slightly. "Sacrifice, indeed," the cardinal said, "but a fitting monument to God's glory."

"God's glory doesn't live in monuments," Aadam responded.

Cardinal Amato was anxious to switch gears. "The Pope is finishing up a meeting. Can I get you anything? Water? Coffee?"

Sol and Burke both shook their heads.

Cardinal Amato turned to the boy. "Anything for you, Aadam?

Aadam thought for a moment. "Do you have any Red Bull?" he finally asked.

The elderly cardinal raised a brow.

THE VAULTED CORRIDORS of the Papal Palace were even more garish than the ones Aadam was escorted through earlier. Aadam sipped on a large can of Red Bull eyeing the gold statues, massive paintings and the other trappings of Catholic wealth with dismay.

Amato escorted the group through a final narrow corridor towards the outer Papal Offices. As Aadam passed a large window, he caught sight of a massive crowd assembling outside.

"They've come to see the Pope?" Aadam asked Amato still sipping on his Red Bull.

"They've come to see you," replied Amato.

Aadam stared at Sol slightly overwhelmed as they finally reached the last set of wooden doors behind which the most powerful man in Christendom received his visitors.

A FRAIL OCTOGENARIAN propped up in a chair by a large fireplace, his head bowed in prayer, looked up calmly as the entourage entered. The Pope rose slowly as the group moved closer to greet him.

"Your Holiness, may I present Arthur Burke, Sol Turner and of course—Aadam Samuel James," Amato said with an unnecessary flourish. The Pope tolerated Amato. Amato was ruthlessly political and politics were a necessary evil in a world where the Pope no longer ruled with an iron hand like the emperor-popes of old. Still, he and Amato were polar opposites. At 86 Pope Clement suffered from various physical failings, but he never failed to be, first and foremost, a man of God. Amato was a man beholden to a Machiavellian pragmatism. But each man had his destiny. Pope Clement was certain of this, even more so now that he was in the presence of the boy.

"Welcome and bless you all," he said with a grandfatherly kindness. The Pope clasped hands warmly with all of them. Aadam stared into the

Pope's eyes, intrigued with his inner peace.

"Please ...," The Pope motioned Aadam to sit on the couch. The boy complied. Burke started over to a chair. The Pope tilted his head slightly to the side halting Burke's advance

"I would like some time alone with Aadam so we can get to know one another," the Pope said to Burke apologetically. Then the Pope turned to Sol asking, "Is this permissible?"

"Certainly, Sir—I mean, Your *Holiness,*" Sol answered clumsily.

"Thank you," the Pope said as he proceeded to sit across from Aadam on the couch.

Burke seemed disappointed he wouldn't be in on the meeting but Sol nodded firmly that they should both make their way outside. Burke reluctantly complied and the doors shut quietly behind them leaving the Pope and Aadam alone on the sofa in front of the fire.

The Pope studied Aadam while the boy took in the room—especially the large crucifix above the fireplace. Aadam felt oddly at ease there. Familiar. The Pope sensed all this.

"I'm glad you saw fit to come," he told the boy.

Aadam watched the Pope a moment. Especially the Pope's eyes—sage-like, but covered over with a pale, milky hue.

"You have served tirelessly," Aadam said softly.

"Yet I am tired," the Pope said quietly.

"From pushing against the immovable."

"You refer to the stubbornness of man?"

"Yes," Aadam answered.

The Pope studied the boy; open to his words and, in the deepest sense, hoping they came from a higher place.

"In your heart, how have we failed?" he asked Aadam.

"The absence of example," Aadam replied without hesitation. "Millions go hungry while the custodians of this Church live in luxury."

"Historically, we saw this as the way to inspire. To lift them up."

"Yet it is clear they remain oppressed."

"And how would you change this?" the Pope asked sincerely.

"I would give that which was given to God to those whom God loves equally," Aadam replied.

"To all men?"

"To all those in *need*. When the needy cease to need all men benefit."

"You would give away that which belongs to the Church?" the Pope asked.

Aadam moved closer to the Pope as he answered. "The Church possesses nothing but the duty to provide for the needs of its members, faithful *and* unfaithful—sinners and saints."

Aadam's words seemed to resonate with the old Pope. The Pope leaned back on the sofa both contemplative and tired. Aadam took the Pope's hand and put it softly between his own.

ON THE STEPS of St. Peter's, Sol stared up at the imposing monument to Christianity. In his own mind, he was killing time, waiting for the meeting between Aadam and the Pope to finish. But there was something more at work in that moment. He stood outside the centuries-old basilica finding it difficult to summon the courage to go inside as he had promised his wife. Two South Korean Nuns passed him as he lingered on the steps. One of them dropped her rosary unaware. Sol retrieved it and chased after them to return it. By the time he caught up to them, he found himself inside the massive cathedral surrounded by hundreds of pilgrims and tourists.

The nuns nodded gratefully and left him alone in a vestibule beneath St. Peter's vaulted ceilings of gold. A choir sang softly at an altar. Sol eyed the candles at their side. He fished in his pockets for the money he would leave to light one. And as he walked towards them through the towering basilica, a feeling came over him. He ignored it at first, struggling with the instinctive contempt he carried for places like these but St. Peter's had an unyielding power. The incense, choir and ringing steeple bells caused Sol to finally relent and let the magnitude of his surroundings have their way with him.

JUST A FEW miles away inside Rome's Hotel de la Ville above the Spanish Steps, an American pilot in uniform opened the door of his suite. A blond waiter wheeled in a room service cart with his lunch. The pilot signed the bill and the waiter left.

As the waiter made his way down the hotel corridor, he pushed the room service cart into a maintenance closet and stealthily slipped through a door that led to the stairs. As he bounded down the stairs towards the hotel's rear service entrance, the *waiter* removed his white waiter's jacket and stuffed it into the trash chute on the staircase landing. He proceeded to make his way outside.

INSIDE THE PAPAL office, the Pope was spellbound sitting in his chair watching Aadam who was *writhing* violently on the floor having another one of his seizures. The sight of this crippled the old Pope at first, but he got hold of himself and moved over to put a gentle hand on Aadam's forehead.

The boy's body finally stopped convulsing and it came to rest on the marble floor. Aadam recovered, finding compassion and wonder in the Pope's eyes.

"Sorry," Aadam said embarrassed. "This happens to me sometimes. I don't know why."

"It is the power of the spirit trapped in a flesh that cannot hold it," the Pope marveled as Aadam sat back up on the couch disoriented. "I am grateful to have witnessed this day," the Pope continued. "I have but one thing to ask."

"Anything," the boy replied.

"Hear my confession?" said the Pope with a frail desperation in his eyes.

Aadam nodded softly.

AS THE MOMENT passed between the seventeen-year-old boy and the eighty-six-year-old Pope, Sol was still inside St. Peter's sitting in a pew in front of the *five* candles he lit for his son. He would have lit more but there were none left. He struggled internally with the formation of a *prayer* to make good on the promise he made to his wife. The five candles he lit were grouped together as if somehow they could unite into a single miracle.

Sol turned to find a very old Italian priest staring at him. The priest gently motioned Sol forward. Sol didn't know what to make of this at first, and then he understood. Sol reluctantly knelt on the padded plank beneath him. And as he closed his eyes, he waited for something— the elusive *prayer* to come to him. Eventually, something indescribable came over him and for a moment a murmur of peace washed over him until suddenly his cellphone rang loudly sparking protest from the others kneeling around him. He quickly jumped up apologizing with his hands to the congregation as he answered.

"This is Turner," he whispered into the phone as he headed outside. Then he realized he was the recipient of some really bad news. "What?! … You're kidding me?! … I'll be right there!" Shaken, he ended the call and raced down the basilica's steps towards the Papal Palace in the distance.

IN THE CORRIDOR outside the Papal Offices, Burke was waiting for Sol as he finally made his way back.

"What happened?!" Sol asked Burke, gasping for breath after taking five flights of steps on the run.

"Aadam said the Pope was speaking to him and just ... the Pope just collapsed."

Burke opened the door. He and Sol went inside, finding Aadam and Amato standing near the couch watching a Vatican doctor administer to Pope Clement. The Pope was barely conscious, lying prostrate on the sofa. He turned frailly towards the group hovering over him and said softly, "Please don't make a fuss over me. It is nothing."

Amato turned to the group. "Pope Clement will be fine but I would like to clear the room until we can stabilize him."

Sol nodded. He and Burke started to leave. So did Aadam, but he stopped suddenly and went over to whisper something in the Pope's ear. Whatever he whispered seemed to calm the ailing Pope. He clasped Aadam's hand gently saying goodbye with his eyes. He released the boy's hand and Aadam finally left the room.

Outside in the corridor, Sol was probing Cardinal Amato about the Pope's illness. "How long has he been sick?"

Amato seemed anxious to minimize the

gravity of the situation. "I'm sure it's just a temporary—"

"Cardinal, I know a sick man when I see one," Sol pressed.

Amato finally replied reluctantly, "This has been going on over a year."

"Is it serious?" asked Burke.

"None of us know," Amato answered. "It's best we let him rest."

"Let him have his sherry," Aadam said to Amato's surprise.

"He mentioned the wine to you?"

"No," Aadam replied. "But it comforts him."

Cardinal Amato stared at the boy unnerved for a moment, and then nodded.

"Thank you all for coming," Amato finally told the group, anxious to get back to the ailing Pope. "He was so much looking forward to it."

They said their goodbyes and the Vatican aides escorted them out. Amato looked after Aadam unsettled; something was either very wrong or very right. At the moment, the cardinal was unsure. The visitors disappeared around the corridor out of his sight. Before he returned to the Pope's side, he pulled out his cellphone to make a phone call. He was careful to do so out of sight of his secretary in the background and he dialed quickly with a newfound sense of urgency. The cardinal was behaving strangely. It would pale in the face of the strangeness to come.

Chapter VIII

The G5 still had its ramp down on the tarmac at Rome Fiumicino Airport. Aadam and Burke were already on board getting settled for their flight back across the Atlantic to Washington. Sol made sure the perimeter was clear and security was tight before boarding. Twenty armed carabinieri surrounded the G5 and their commanding officer gave Sol the all clear sign over his radio. Sol finally made his way up the ramp to board. As he did, the Captain poked his head out to greet him.

"We good in there?" Sol asked.

"Minor complication," the Pilot answered. "Our co-pilot came down with a bad case of food poisoning at the hotel."

"We're flying without a co-pilot?!"

"No, no. We're good. His substitute flies for the State Department. He'll be fine," the Pilot assured him.

Sol nodded and looked inside the cockpit. The new co-pilot greeted Sol with a smile and a thumbs-up. It was the blond man who delivered the room service cart to the American pilot at the Hotel De La Ville in Rome. Only this time he was wearing the uniform of a pilot instead of a waiter. This bit of information would have been helpful for Sol to have. Without it, Sol just nodded politely at the substitute not knowing how much he would regret that as he made his way back to his seat in the rear of the plane.

The G5's turbines revved and, in seconds, it made its way down the runway and powered into the sky.

AS THE G5 punched through the clouds above Italy, Sol wandered past Aadam who was seated off to the side deeply absorbed. Aadam was writing in the small leather-bound book he had written in earlier.

Burke was in the back reading. Sol sat down beside him. Burke closed his book. Sol eyed its cover and read its title—*Scientific Perspectives on Divine Action*

"A gift from Amato?" Sol asked.

"The Vatican book shop," Burke replied." "They sponsored five conferences where scientists and theologians debated the epistemological evidence for the existence of God."

"And?"

"The evidence was powerful. If I were a religious man—"

"But as a scientist?"

Burke considered his answer a moment before he gave it. "As a scientist, I probably would have called Jesus a fraud."

"Then what makes you think he wasn't?"

"The Resurrection."

"A myth invented by apostles horrified that the Romans managed to kill him," was Sol's dismissal.

"No," Burke responded adamantly. "Think about it? The Romans crucified him as a deterrent, to force Christians to disavow a religion disloyal to the throne and the head rabbis of the time condoned it, believing the Nazarene was heretical and a threat to their hegemony. His followers were terrified and fled denouncing him as the Messiah to ensure their survival. It wasn't until he actually started *appearing* to the Apostles, to hundreds, according to Paul, that the Christians came out into the open again. They were tortured and murdered yet their faith was unshaken. In those early years after the crucifixion, hundreds, maybe even thousands lost their lives refusing to renounce him. No mere *myth* would have inspired that kind of loyalty."

"Sorry. Don't buy it," Sol said cynically.

"Well, perhaps if you ever see a dead man walking, you might change your mind," Burke said with a smile.

Sol laughed. But his laugh was short-lived as he jumped up from his seat feeling the plane bank *hard right*.

Burke looked at Sol rattled. "Why are we turning?"

Sol didn't answer, he was too busy moving towards the cockpit passing through the middle cabin where he drew his gun quickly seeing his two other agents *dead* on the cabin floor.

A shot rang out from behind him. Sol hit the floor grabbing the slice of flesh that had just been ripped from his shoulder from the bullet fired from the blond co-pilot's .40 handgun.

The pilot went for the kill. He lunged at Sol but Sol was quick and managed to swing his leg underneath him. The co-pilot was knocked off-balance. Sol quickly jumped to his feet and tackled the co-pilot, viciously pounding his fist into the blond man's face.

The co-pilot jabbed three fingers into Sol's eye. Sol jerked back in pain. The co-Pilot grabbed the gun that Sol had kicked out of his hand and by the time Sol regained his vision, he found the .40 aimed at his face.

"Make it easy on yourself. All I want is the

boy," the co-Pilot said icily. "We land in Istanbul and you go free. Or die here, you decide."

Sol made his calculations as the co-pilot motioned him to sit. The co-pilot had already fired one well-placed shot that had missed and buried itself in the sofa in the middle cabin. One more misplaced shot would increase the odds of putting a hole in the outer fuselage and depressurizing the cabin. Sol sat down deciding he would let this play out a little and wait for the right moment to take the co-pilot down. The last thing Sol expected was that the moment would come from Burke until he heard—"Strap in, Turner!" as Burke yelled from the rear.

The pilot spun around as Sol strapped his seat belt down hard. The blond man rushed into the rear cabin and found Burke strapped to a seat by the G5's door which he was ready to slide open. The blond man raised his weapon but—*WWOOOSSHH*. Too late. The door jerked open and the cabin depressurized. The blond man struggled to keep his grip on the handrail, his body floating in air, the depressurized cabin ripping him outwards.

Burke, struggling to breathe, managed to break the blond man's grip, and the remainder of the co-pilot's body was sucked violently outside.

Burke watched as the hijacker plunged 30,000 feet to his death.

Burke turned to Aadam who was strapped in his seat, struggling to breathe. Burke fought with the mechanism to close door. The vacuum was too much to overcome. Burke couldn't do it. Aadam focused all his concentration on the door, his face contorting. Suddenly, the door seemed to move, just enough that Burke could finally ratchet it shut. Burke grabbed the oxygen mask which had dropped from the ceiling in front of them. He gulped air from it, then placed it over Aadam's face.

"You okay?!" he asked the boy.

Aadam nodded. Burke moved quickly into the forward cabin where he found Sol using a fire extinguisher to bash in the locked door to the cockpit.

As Burke arrived, Sol was looking at the course of the G5's autopilot.

"Good job back there. The kid okay?" Sol said to Burke feeling him come up behind him.

"Yeah, the kid's okay"

"We got a little problem," Sol said, eyeing the G5's captain slumped over dead in the pilot's seat. He was strangled by his own tie.

Burke pulled out the captain's body from his seat and squeezed his own body in behind the controls.

Sol watched, encouraged. "Don't tell me you can fly one of these things?"

"I flew F4s in 'Nam. You get me on with a tower, they'll talk us down."

Sol studied Burke a moment, the *psychiatrist* now morphed into this fiercely determined fighter, one inhumanly calm under pressure. Unfortunately, Sol didn't have time to dwell on it. "Closest American Base is Aviano," Sol told him.

"Fine. Get 'em on the com."

Sol grabbed the radio mic as Burke released the G5 from autopilot.

AN HOUR LATER, after the tower's lead controller at the U.S. Air Force Base in Aviano managed to talk Burke through a 30,000-foot descent and an approach to the tarmac, the G5 was finally ready to attempt a landing. Fire and rescue crews were standing by as the G5 knifed downwards through the clouds above the base.

Burke managed to guide the G5 towards the asphalt. The landing was rough but the two F-16s that had escorted the G5 back climbed sharply seeing the G5 safely on the runway. The fire and rescue vehicles raced towards it, sirens blaring, as it taxied safely to a stop.

Aviano crewmen quickly rolled up a ramp to the G5's front door. As it swung open, Air Force MPs raced up the ramp. Aadam was the first out. The MPs hustled him off to an armored Suburban waiting below.

Sol was out next, already on his cellphone with Larson, who was in his FBI offices in D.C. Both were deeply agitated.

"How the hell could we miss this?!" Sol screamed into his cell.

Larson's office was humming with fifty agents scouring for intel in the background as he responded, "The pilot's ID checked out. By the time we realized it was a forgery you guys were already airborne and, unbeknownst to you, he had obviously severed the com link."

Sol threw up his hands, watching Burke finally exit the plane. "I don't care, Larson! The guy *slipped through*! Dammit, Frank, the kid— we almost lost him!"

"Look, he's safe. That's all that matters," Larson replied into his cell. "He might not be our jurisdiction now anyway."

"Might not be our … What are you talking about?"

Larson finally realized Sol didn't know. "Didn't you hear the news out of the Vatican?"

"No."

"Pope Clement died an hour ago. His last words were about the kid."

Sol took a moment to react. Finally—"Okay … And?"

"He wants him to be the next Pope."

Sol just hung there floored. Aadam looked up at him from the tarmac as he was herded into the armored Suburban with Burke. The two locked eyes a moment before Aadam was whisked away.

Chapter IX

Outside Aadam's brownstone safe house in Washington, fifty Secret Service agents and local police encircled a barricaded, three block perimeter.

On the building's third floor, Burke moved down a corridor speaking into his cell escorted by two Secret Service agents, "I don't know how we can keep his whereabouts a secret with this army you've got out there."

Sol was on his cell inside the FBI offices alongside Larson. "That *army* is half what we need," he told Burke. "We have no idea what we're up against. How is he?"

Burke hovered outside the door to Aadam's apartment. "He's safely inside."

Behind the apartment door, Aadam was alone on his knees in front of a fireplace in the otherwise darkened room. His head bowed in prayer, his face was filled with a curious mix of piety and confusion. A palpable heaviness overwhelmed him as he stared mesmerized at the flames.

IT WAS 2 A.M. and Sol was still inside the FBI offices trying to put all the pieces together. He was beat but he needed to figure out who was trying to kill the boy in his charge and why. And he needed to do it fast. Audio from a TV newscast playing in the background bled into his thoughts as he hovered in front of a large bulletin board filled with pictures of the suspects.

"Another EU bank declared insolvency today further straining the funding mechanism of the ECB," the newscaster declared as Sol moved the picture of the blond man to a group of other pictures tacked under a picture of a Muslim sheikh. The blond man didn't seem to fit with the others in the group. Sol focused, desperate to find linkage as the newscast continued.

"… All eyes are on the G20 summit next week, where world leaders will struggle to find solutions for the institutional collapse, record unemployment, and rioting around the globe."

Sol turned to the TV. He watched the newscast cut to a flurry of violent protests erupting in city after city—a world ripping itself apart.

The newscaster continued, "… On his deathbed last night, Pope Clement referred to us as *a world in desperate need of a savior …"* The newscast's footage cut to archival footage of

Aadam and Sol as their entourage tried to duck the hounding press at Andrews Air Force Base after they arrived from Aviano earlier in the day. Over these images the announcer continued, "... As Aadam Samuel James arrives back in Washington after yet another assassination attempt, we can't help but ask ourselves—has the pontiff found our answer?"

Sol's cellphone rang suddenly, startling him. He turned down the TV. "Turner," he said into his cell.

Anne was in bed inside her apartment. "You still up?"

"Yeah. I called the hospital. He was out of his room. How's—"

"He couldn't sleep so we took him outside. He needed to get out of that bed," she answered. "So tell me, did you ask Aadam if he could help Michael?"

"You mean while the hijacker was trying to shoot me or while he was having his one on one with the Pope?" Sol replied irritated.

Anne realized immediately that she should have been more sympathetic to what he must be going through. "Look, I'm not trying to fight, I'm only—?

"Don't worry about it. I'm just on edge. And for what it's worth, I asked him."

"Well, what did he say?"

Sol grew even more frustrated. "Anne, I wasn't looking for an answer, okay? I just told him you wanted me to mention it."

"You should have pressed it. He'll have no time if they elect him Pope—"

"Elect him?!" Sol barked back cynically. "He'll never get through the College of Cardinals. Half those sharks spent their lives clawing for that job. No way. It just won't happen."

"Why are you always so negative? Why can't you at least acknowledge that he may be the One?"

Sol stared at the images of violent riots still flashing on the TV before he answered, "Because there isn't a *One*, Anne. There's only *us*— confused and rudderless, fighting to navigate the storm."

"You're hopeless, you know that, don't you? How many miracles will it take to convince you?"

"I don't know. How many you got?"

Anne responded with dial tone. Sol pocketed his cellphone frustrated. He resumed studying images of the terrorists while images of a massive crowd gathering outside the Vatican played on the TV.

Chapter X

Father Grimaldi stared at that same massive crowd out his window in the offices at the Vatican.

Outside, thousands waved signs urging the cardinals to elect Aadam as their next Pope. Grimaldi picked up a file and straightened his hair. Palpably nervous, he gathered his wits and headed out of his office.

Inside the Sistine Chapel, Cardinal Amato was speaking at the head of the conclave gathered together to determine the Pope elect. He was deep in a heated conversation with the other cardinals as Father Grimaldi entered through a side door.

" ... Our mandate from the Apostolic Convention is clear." Amato lectured the other cardinals while reading from a Vatican rules book. *"The cardinal electors are not to allow their choice to be guided by friendship or aversion, by influence or favor, by force, fear or the pursuit of popularity. Rather, having before their eyes solely the glory of God and the Church, they shall give their vote to the person, even 'outside' the College of Cardinals, who in their judgment is 'most suited' to govern the universal Church in a fruitful and beneficial way."* Amato closed the book and looked out over the sea of reluctant cardinals in the conclave.

"He's a *child*. Barely a deacon," protested one of the cardinals. "How can he rule? What can he know?"

"The will of God!" another cardinal yelled.

Amato finally turned to Father Grimaldi. Grimaldi knew the moment would come, but the weight of it still crippled him.

"Father," Amato bellowed: "Are you prepared to submit your final report?"

All eyes moved to Grimaldi, the humble priest in their midst. Grimaldi chose his words carefully. "Yes, Eminence. But with ... with reservation."

Amato was taken aback, but he forced himself to conceal his displeasure. "In regards to what, Father Grimaldi?"

"The boy's origin," Grimaldi answered meekly. "A woman contacted me this morning with knowledge of his past. And ... and there seems to be a discrepancy."

"Well, what is it? Enlighten us?" Amato said impatiently.

"She will only speak of it in person, Eminence," Grimaldi answered.

"And where is this woman?"

"Pennsylvania," Grimaldi answered, knowing how his answer would spark murmurs in the crowd.

Amato eyed the noisy populist crowd out the Vatican windows, and then he turned back to Grimaldi forcefully. "Well, get on a plane. They are restless. We must give them a Pope!"

Grimaldi nodded reluctantly, feeling the weight of the world suddenly on his shoulders.

AT DULLES AIRPORT, the international terminal was barely awake as Grimaldi faced the conclave. Dulles' first group of trans-Atlantic passengers had just disembarked. Rabbi Rossen was among them. He retrieved his luggage from the baggage carousel and headed outside.

It was a cold winter's dawn in Washington as a Hertz agent wearing a yarmulke escorted Rossen to his rental vehicle and handed him the keys. The agent left and Rossen opened the trunk of the rental car. He seemed satisfied with the cache of automatic weapons inside. He shut the trunk and drove away.

LARSON ARRIVED EARLY to FBI headquarters that same morning. He poked his head into the conference room where Sol had pulled an all-nighter pouring through intel on the suspected assassins. Larson handed Sol a latte and cinnamon roll. Sol nodded gratefully.

"You got a phone call," Larson said, nodding to a bank of phones on the table.

Sol picked up the only flashing line.

THE DNI'S OFFICE was nondescript and furnished minimally. As Director of National Intelligence, Simon Novak wasn't concerned with furnishings or style; he was only interested in results. And Novak knew Sol was spending a lot of time at the FBI rather than focusing on his normal duties at Secret Service. Novak wasn't happy about this and Sol was the recipient of his wrath. " ... Look, I get it, Turner, but the agency has better uses for your time," Novak said firmly into his phone.

"Sir, we're making progress—"

"—I'm in the loop on all of it, Turner. But Larson can handle it. He's FBI, you're not anymore, remember?" Novak said irritated. "Now I want you with the kid."

"Sir, we've got fifty men around him. His detail's bigger than the President's!" Sol fired back frustrated.

"The kid wants *you*," Novak answered firmly.

"I'm flattered but I can serve *better* here. By finding out who's trying to kill him!"

"Turner, in case you hadn't noticed I am *not* asking. It's an order from P.O.T.U.S. The kid's got a big day ahead of him—a *billion* people are going to meet him."

"What? Where?"

"Biggest church on the planet—" Novak answered—"Keisha."

"Keisha?!" Sol was unnerved. Keisha Jackson was a five-time Grammy winning recording artist before she became the world's most famous daytime talk show host. Her live audiences broke records, sometimes 50,000 strong. And Sol knew any one of them could be Aadam's next assassin.

THE WASHINGTON BROWNSTONE that had become Aadam's temporary residence was still surrounded by the previous fifty-man detail but Sol had added an armored SWAT team van to round out the arsenal. No one was allowed in or out of that building without Sol's approval. As Sol made his way up the stairway towards Aadam's apartment, he checked in with his agents at their posts. His cellphone rang.

"Turner," Sol said sharply into his phone thinking it might be Larson with some breaking intel.

It wasn't Larson. It was Anne. And she was beside herself. "Sol, something's wrong with Michael! Jergens just called from the hospital. Michael's having trouble breathing. Jergens sounded like he was in a panic about it. I'm going down there now!"

"Shit," Sol replied unnerved. His mind raced. Not that there could ever be a perfect time for this news, but it certainly wasn't now. He was stuck there, the President insisting that it be so, and he was pissed about it but he tried to stay calm for her. "Okay ... I'm sure they'll get a handle on it. But I'll get down there. Somehow, I'll get down there."

"Come now, please!" she begged.

Sol spotted Aadam moving down the hall towards him escorted by five Secret Service agents. Sol's heart sank. "I can't right now. But I'll get there. I promise."

"Dammit, Sol, this is your son!" she yelled, trying to fight back the tears.

"Dammit, I know that!" he said in a harsh whisper as Aadam's entourage was almost on top of him. "I will get *there*!" were his last words to Anne before he hung up. Aadam was inches from him now, accompanied by Burke.

"Good morning," Aadam said warmly.

"Morning." Sol's response was clipped and everybody noticed. Sol didn't care. He motioned the group to the elevator doors. In seconds, the entourage was moving through the lobby making their way to the armored government Suburbans outside.

As Aadam's heavily escorted caravan wound through the streets of Washington towards the studio where Keisha would broadcast her landmark special to the world, Sol was preoccupied and staring numbly out the window.

Aadam noticed and seemed unsettled by it. "What's wrong?"

"My son can't breathe," Sol replied without turning.

"Then you should be with him."

Sol finally turned and unloaded on the kid. "Yeah, well, I know that. But we got a date with *Keisha*.'"

"She can wait," Aadam said firmly.

Burke intervened. "Nonsense. This is a major opportunity for Aadam—".

"It can wait," Aadam said defiantly. "Sol's son is fighting for his life."

Burke squirmed "Aadam, I don't think it's

wise to—"

"We *go!*" Aadam said, cutting Burke off.

Aadam nodded to Sol. Sol considered every-thing a beat, had a *screw it* moment inside his head, then signaled the driver to make the de-tour.

Burke was pissed but he would keep that in check for now knowing they would eventually understand the price of crossing him.

ST. JUDE'S HOSPITAL was crowded that morning. A rash of overdoses from the night be-fore added to the chaos caused by Aadam's en-tourage marching down the halls towards the private room at the end.

Anne had no idea what was coming. She was at Michael's side and she looked up startled as Sol barged in flanked by Aadam and two more Secret Service Agents. Sol was shell-shocked seeing Michael in his hospital bed. Michael was inhumanly pale, struggling to breathe, but his face brightened seeing his father.

Frustrated, Sol turned to the nurse on duty. "Where's Dr. Jergens?"

"On his way," the nurse replied.

Sol moved to Michael and grabbed his son's hand while Anne stared at Aadam, humbled by his presence. Michael watched Aadam as he stood calmly in the background.

"How you feeling, champ?" Sol asked Michael gently.

On the monitor behind them, Sol could see Michael's vitals were tanking. Sol could secure a crowd of a hundred thousand; he could leap six feet through the air and take a bullet in the hip while it was traveling at a thousand feet per second like he did for the President, but Sol was at a loss for what to do here. So he settled for the obvious, "Michael, this is Aadam Samuel James."

Aadam smiled warmly. He moved over to Michael and shook the hand that Michael could barely lift. Aadam held it gently while putting his hand on Michael's forehead. He silently mouthed the words of a prayer. Michael seemed to calm.

Dr. Jergens finally arrived, rushing in out of breath.

"Sorry. Got here as soon as I could," He said to Sol apologetically before he noticed Aadam. "Oh, excuse me; I didn't know you were here. I'm Doctor Jergens." Jergens extended his hand.

Aadam shook it, responding, "Hello."

"I'm afraid I'm going to have to ask you all to leave," Jergens told the group politely. "I have to run some tests on your son."

Sol nodded. Both he and Anne said a reluctant goodbye to Michael. Aadam smiled at Michael and nodded goodbye putting his hand once more on Michael's forehead. Michael seemed comforted by his presence. He could barely breathe, each breath weaker than the last, but he was still sad to see Aadam go.

The entourage was waiting outside in the corridor when Aadam emerged from Michael's room. Anne turned to Aadam warmly, "Thank you so much. I am so grateful that you came."

Aadam stared at Anne for a moment, her frailty evident, her grief fighting her panic. And next to her, Sol, this courageous centurion, crippled by the sight of his dying son. Both of them, two halves of a broken marriage.

"Grateful?" Aadam finally replied. "How? Others search their whole lives for the sacred union that you would cast away."

Sol and Anne just hung there. Stung. Bordering on shamed. Burke finally showed up, breaking the moment. He nodded firmly to Sol. Sol had gotten his tiny, though tragic, reprieve. Now it was time to go.

Chapter XI

A Cessna 421 landed at a tiny airport in Lancaster, Pennsylvania.

Father Grimaldi was its sole passenger. A woman approached him, seeing his cassock as he climbed out of the plane with a single piece of luggage. She was mid-30s, rail-thin and tall. Probably an ex-junkie, now just this terrified gazelle.

"Father Grimaldi?" she said, even though the answer was obvious.

"Yes," Grimaldi replied politely. "Carol Hanway?"

The woman nodded, seeming to wish it weren't so. "My car's right outside."

Grimaldi followed her towards the parking lot. There was a sense of urgency in his walk and a sea of apprehension in his eyes.

KEISHA'S MAKESHIFT STUDIO was the biggest any of her crew had ever worked in. They chose the largest convention center in Richmond, Virginia and transformed it into a multi-camera, crane-equipped broadcast extravaganza. A live audience of seventy thousand was in their seats in the auditorium, restless because of the delay but giddy with anticipation. Not just to see Aadam, but to watch Keisha in her element. She surprised the audience with an impromptu performance of her biggest hit, *I Believe, Do You?* which she dedicated to Aadam. Somehow, the spectacle of it all seemed fitting.

A production assistant greeted Sol and Aadam as their entourage moved through a frantic crew preparing backstage.

"Sorry we're late," Sol told the production assistant.

"No worries, it's handled," the PA answered, motioning them towards the makeup room. "Can you come with me?"

Aadam nodded and the PA whisked him away. Sol signaled the other agents to fan out. Twenty Agents backstage morphed into guardian mode coordinating with fifty more working the audience outside

In the make-up room, a make-up artist was feverishly at work on Aadam. Aadam stopped her, uncomfortable with the process. The make-up artist acquiesced and nodded to the PA who whispered something into his radio.

Sol moved to the curtain. Peeked out towards the stage watching Keisha working the audience. She was in an elegant gown, her infectious charisma channeling a rarefied mix of Whitney Houston and Oprah. The audience loved her and she reciprocated genuinely.

"Thank you! It's great to see you! I love you all so much!" her voiced yelled into her mic to thundering applause. "Well, I've just heard our very special guest is ready. Ladies and gentlemen, please join me in giving a warm and grateful welcome to Aadam Samuel James!"

The applause was deafening, as was the thundering boom of fifty thousand people jumping to their feet. Hundreds, if not thousands were crying, two women in the front fainted at the sight of Aadam as he stood there humbly, slightly overwhelmed by the reception.

Keisha crossed over to him and shook his hand. "Hi, I'm Keisha," she said into the mic then moved it in front of Aadam.

"I think I intuited that," Aadam said smiling, accompanied by a roar of laughter from the crowd.

Keisha motioned him to sit. Aadam sat calmly looking out over the sea of admiring faces in the crowd as the applause died down.

"They're very excited to see you," Keisha

said, finally settling into her chair. "How's it feel to be here?"

"Well, if you must know, I'm a little nervous."

"Nervous? Well, aren't we all," she answered to more laughter and applause. "Tell us, Aadam," she continued. "You were one of the last people to see the Pope. What did he say to you?"

Aadam's demeanor grew solemn as he replied. "That the Church was in need."

"And that it needed you?" she answered gently.

"I am just a messenger."

"Then I guess we'd all like to know the message."

"It is as it always was," Aadam replied.

"As in *Ten Commandments*? As in *do unto others*?"

"Yes. All of it."

"Nothing new? Nothing more?" Keisha prodded.

"What was everything cannot become less," Aadam replied. "What diminishes is the faith to follow."

"So without faith, we're doomed, is that it?" she said.

Aadam took a long beat to answer, while the

crowd watched him silent and spellbound. He just stared at her making her shift uncomfortably in her chair. Finally, he responded— "Let's start with *do unto others as you would have them do unto you*. If every breath you take feeds off the truth in those words and your courage to follow them, then no, you are not doomed."

"You're asking us to believe it's that simple?"

"Yes. And to believe otherwise is to ignore the miracle of God's love."

"The miracle of hunger? The miracle of genocide?" she said cynically.

"The failings of men, not God," Aadam responded firmly. "All these things are in man's power to eradicate the moment man chooses God's love over the love of himself."

Backstage, Sol watched Aadam, ever skeptical, but fascinated by the boy's poise and inhuman calm. The production assistant came up behind him talking nervously with someone else on his headset.

Back on stage, Keisha was getting down to the important matter at hand. "Aadam, there are many out there who are calling you the *Messiah*. Are you comfortable with that?"

"Not if I meet the same fate as the last one," he answered wryly.

The crowd erupted in laughter and applause. Keisha smiled, but pressed on. "Seriously though, Aadam, your miracles have convinced a lot of us that you speak from a higher authority. And we're living in desperate times, the apocalypse is on many people's minds, so I have to ask you, have we ... I guess there's no other way to say it—have we come to the *end of days*?"

Aadam stared out a moment at the crowd. There was no laughing now. No applause only faces desperate for guidance, desperate to believe, a longing for hope. The audience was eerily still.

Aadam stood and addressed the crowd—"Is an apocalypse what you seek?"

A few, then suddenly hundreds started chanting *NO! NOT NOW! NEVER!*

Aadam turned pointedly to Sol who he knew was watching from backstage. Then he continued addressing Sol at first before turning back to the crowd—"Then empty your hearts of hatred and vengeance. Fill them with faith." Aadam started walking to the audience as he continued. "Choose sustainability over gluttony!" he boomed, walking down into the crowd as people swarmed around him. "Selflessness over self!" he demanded as the crowd started chanting *YES!*

"God over Godlessness!" Aadam continued as the entire audience rose to their feet. "Know that from the moment of birth it has been in your power and yours *alone* to choose!"

The audience went wild. A thousand people encircled him. Sol was rattled—Aadam was at risk. Sol signaled his men to form a protective barricade around Aadam as suddenly, the production assistant grabbed Sol's shoulder from behind. Sol turned to him on edge but was even more startled by something the production assistant told him. Sol nodded after the production assistant finished and the PA moved quickly on stage and rushed over to Keisha to whisper something in her ear.

Keisha's eyes widened. She grabbed her mic and spoke into it forcefully. "Ladies and gentlemen, please! Quiet! Please, listen a moment!"

The crowd settled. All eyes, including Aadam's were on Keisha now.

"I've just been notified of something profound," she continued. "No. *Miraculous!*" She turned to her PA and asked, "Can you bring him out here?"

The production assistant nodded and headed straight to Sol. Sol watched him confused as the PA grabbed his hand.

"Please, Mr. Turner. Join us!" she said into

the mic to Sol.

"What? Not necessary … no," Sol said but the PA grabbed him by the arm and led Sol reluctantly to the stage as Keisha turned to the crowd.

"Mr. Turner is the agent in charge of protecting Aadam," she told the audience. "And we've just been informed that his son, a young teenager who is battling an incurable disease—" tears welled up in Keisha's eyes as she continued, "—well, after a visit from Aadam, Sol's son, Michael is his name, well, he's completely recovered!" The crowd gasped as she continued. "He's up! Walking! Cured! A hundred percent! The doctors can't believe it!"

The crowd roared. Sol didn't know what to do. Half of him didn't want to believe but the other half was desperate for a miracle. Suddenly, in the commotion, Sol's cellphone rang.

"Go ahead, Mr. Turner. Answer it," Keisha prodded.

Sol fumbled for his cell. "… Hello?"

Anne was in the hospital with Michael standing strong and getting dressed beside her.

"Sol, he's healed!" She said crying into her cellphone. "Aadam cured him! He's completely fine!"

She handed her phone to Michael. "Dad?"

Michael said euphorically.

Back onstage, Keisha and the crowd were silent as Sol tried to hear his son. "Michael?!"

"Dad? Dad, please thank Aadam!"

Sol was completely overwhelmed. "Michael, are you okay?!"

"I'm just perfect. I'm fine. I'm really fine. Just believe it. It happened. Aadam healed me. Are *you* okay?"

Sol just stood there numbly for a moment, trying to stop from shaking. Finally—"Yeah, Champ, I'm ok. I'm just on Keisha."

The crowd laughed.

Michael was laughing too, as he eyed the broadcast on the television in his room. "Yeah, well *duh*, Dad. I know. I can see you."

Sol started to laugh himself but it couldn't stop the tears welling up in his eyes. He fought them back standing there, the whole audience watching him. Sol didn't know what to do. Aadam began walking towards him.

Sol called out to him, "Michael's fine. He's just ... he's fine!"

Aadam started to tear up himself seeing Sol standing on stage naked with emotion. A few people in the crowd began chanting. The chanting turned into a roar as all fifty-thousand audi-

ence members joined in accompanied by countless millions of viewers watching around the
world—all of them in unison chanting the
name—

Aadam! Aadam! Aadam! Aadam!

Chapter XII

Mountville was a quaint but infinitesimally small town in upstate Pennsylvania. The kind of town that you could easily get lost trying to find, or, if you lived there, stay lost trying not to be found. Carol Hanway's house there was both and its resident was certainly the latter. Father Grimaldi was saying goodbye to Carol as an almost disturbing crimson sun was setting on Mountville, a fitting backdrop for the conversation with a woman who had turned his entire world upside down.

"I'll need you to corroborate this at some point," he warned Carol.

Carol was uneasy. It was a tough decision she had made to contact Grimaldi and she was already regretting it. "Under the circumstances, I don't know if I can do that," Carol said sharply.

"Pray on it," Grimaldi said gently. "The strength will come."

Grimaldi nodded a nervous goodbye and headed for a taxi which waited for him across the street.

RABBI ROSSEN WATCHED TV with more than his usual paranoia. He was holed up inside a small rent-by-the-week apartment on the outskirts of Richmond, Virginia. Dressed in jeans and a t-shirt, Rossen had forsaken his rabbinical gown. And as he clutched a 9mm with one hand and a glass of Jack Daniels with the other, it was clear he had forsaken his rabbinical creed. He studied the images on his television as the banner beneath the image of two announcers debating on the broadcast streamed: *Cardinals Debate Selection of New Pope.*

Onscreen, the anchor posed the question on everyone's minds to his panel, "So how would you handicap his chances?"

The first pundit on the panel squirmed before finally giving his answer, "Well, *if* you believe the Messiah is walking on earth again, how do you elect a cardinal, a mere mortal, to head the Church?"

"That's a big *if,*" the announcer replied.

"Well, for millions of Christians out there marching in the streets, their numbers growing massively day by day, it's not a question of *if* anymore, it's a matter of *fact*," the Pundit countered.

Brooding, and visibly disturbed, Rossen

poured himself another shot of Jack Daniels as the broadcast's footage cut to the Vatican and the hundreds of thousands of Christians gathering beneath St. Peter's.

IF THE SISTINE CHAPEL was a testament to the agony and the ecstasy of Michelangelo, then the conclave of the College of Cardinals convening inside it was a testament to the sheer political will of men who had spent their whole lives jockeying for the highest position in the Catholic Church. The papal throne was at stake and Cardinal Amato was hard at work debating the unconvinced.

"... I'm not disparaging our qualified candidates, but it's incumbent on us—"

"—But we do not know his past!" an angry cardinal from Poland interrupted.

A cardinal from South Africa intervened, "Was not Jesus unknown until his thirties? His hidden years a mystery? Fuel for a millennia of speculation? But his *past* was unimportant. It was his *deeds*, his ability to inspire!"

"And *inspire* is what this boy does!" Amato reinforced. "Aadam has restored hope. Belief has risen up in unbelievers. He is the voice of change. I dare say the voice of God!"

"But our vote must be founded on certitude!" insisted the cardinal from Poland.

"No!" answered Amato forcefully. "It must be founded on *faith*, the foundation of divine allegiance!"

Cardinal Amato began circling the crowd, his vocal intensity building, going in for the close. "My brothers, we are at a turning point, a tipping point. If ever we needed a uniter, it is now! We drown in the quagmire of economic inequality, terrorism and religious division. If ever a man was destined to be the solution to this, it is Aadam Samuel James! Our beloved Pope Clement saw this immediately. His dying wish cannot be discounted. Our duty is clear. Anything less would be spitting in the face of God's will!"

There were a few loud affirmations and roughly the same amount of dissenting murmurs. The cardinals were clearly divided. The arguments continued as Amato's aide came into the chapel and whispered something to Amato. The cardinal followed him outside.

Minutes later, on the phone in his office, Amato paced behind his desk, the news he was hearing was decidedly unpleasant. "... This is conjecture, not empirical proof!" he told Father Grimaldi firmly.

Grimaldi was on his cell outside a post office in Mountville arguing with the cardinal. "But, your Eminence, it is clear that the child may not have been brought to Father Haines as they described!"

"Father Grimaldi," Amato replied, "we're on the verge of an historic vote. Time is short, the faithful *need* a leader. And a leader, the faithful shall have. Nonetheless, I will include your report in the record."

"Eminence, I implore you to consider it before you vote," Grimaldi pleaded.

"You may consider it considered," Amato said dismissively. "Thank you for your efforts and have a safe trip back." Amato hung up the phone.

Clearly troubled, Amato moved to the window and stared out over the heavily manicured Vatican grounds. He eyed the imposing paintings of former Popes lining the walls of his office and considered something before picking up the phone and starting to dial.

IT WAS RAINING outside the White House that morning. The President had his back to it signing documents at his desk while watching a CNN report on TV in the Oval Office.

Onscreen, a reporter stood in the midst of the

massive crowd outside St. Peters. "The cardinals are sequestered," the reporter informed, "no cellphones, tablets or laptops allowed ...

A few miles away, inside his familiar brownstone safe house, Aadam sat on the sofa alongside Burke watching that same broadcast as the CNN reporter onscreen continued, "... when white smoke rises from the dome of the Sistine Chapel, the world will have its new Pope ..."

The FBI Offices across town had the same broadcast playing on its monitors. Sol and Larson were huddled near the bulletin board beneath it as they focused on an enlarged photo of a bearded Arab cleric crossing a street in Pakistan. Larson pointed to the cleric, "That's Sheikh Ansari an hour ago."

Sol eyed the rest of the photos of the suspected terrorist on the bulletin board. Ansari's face was at the top. Underneath Ansari, there were photos of the other extremists and the blond pilot that hijacked the G5.

"Our guys ready to bring us the head of a bearded sheikh?" Sol asked.

Larson nodded confidently.

"Then trigger it," Sol answered icily, anxious for revenge.

Larson grabbed a phone and 7,000 miles

away in the alleys of Lahore, Pakistan, two ol-ive-skinned CIA operatives answered Larson's call. The black ops leader received the *GO* order while his CIA covert operative partner prepped his weapons for Ansari's assassination.

THE CONCLAVE CONTINUED well into the evening. It was finally time to test the pow-ers of Amato's persuasion. The mood was sol-emn as he and the rest of the cardinals began to cast their ballots.

Billions of faithful and unfaithful alike awaited the result, including Father Grimaldi who was inside his taxi on his way to Lancaster airport listening to a news broadcast about the conclave on the taxi's radio.

The taxi was at a flashing stop sign in front of railroad tracks on a rural road cutting through a dense forest. A train was passing in front of them as a blue sedan pulled up behind them. Fa-ther Grimaldi didn't notice. He was too busy looking down at his cellphone, scrolling through names on his contact list. But the sun's glare through the window was too bright to see the screen so he leaned down into the shadows of the back seat to read it as a sharp *fffffftttt* sound accompanied a bullet which pierced the rear window. Grimaldi lurched back in his seat unglued eyeing the driver who had a fresh red hole in the back of his head. Grimaldi freaked as two more bullets pierced the back windshield.

Grimaldi curled up on the floor as the roar of the train subsided when it finally cleared the intersection. The stop sign stopped flashing and the drop gate rose. Grimaldi heaved himself into the front. He pushed the dead driver to the side and floored the accelerator. The taxi barreled through the drop gate and roared down the asphalt. The blue sedan followed. Grimaldi looked in his rear view at the gunman who fired another shot into his window.

As the chase in Lancaster continued, a distinguished gray-haired man was ushered into the Oval Office. The President rose to greet the man reverentially. Whoever this man was, President McCormick clearly saw him as an equal.

More images from the crowd gathered outside the Vatican flashed across the President's TV as the two men sat on the sofa to watch it.

"We're still waiting for any sign of smoke," the CNN reporter onscreen informed his viewers. "The cardinals are taking a long time to make their decision, a decision that might elevate Aadam James to the papal throne. If they

choose him, Aadam would be the second youngest Pope in the Church's history, second only to
Pope Benedict the Ninth, who was rumored to
be twelve or thirteen years old when he took the
throne ..."

Across town, inside the brownstone safe
house, the CNN broadcast continued on the television in the living room as Aadam stared out
his window at a sea of reporters and a massive
crowd of onlookers whom the police were holding back behind a barricade. Aadam turned back
to the broadcast. Burke was still on the sofa
glued to it as the CNN reporter at the Vatican
continued—"I've just gotten word we might be
seeing something soon ... There!" CNN cut to
images of the basilica and the *white smoke* rising
from it. The crowd outside the Vatican went
wild, screaming and cheering as the announcer
continued, "White smoke rising! The cardinals
have decided! The white smoke means they've
finally come to an agreement on the Church's
next Pope!"

The white smoke above the Vatican was decidedly lighter than the white smoke bursting
out the exhaust of Grimaldi's taxi as he continued to drive at high speed in and out of traffic to
evade the blue sedan relentlessly pursuing him.

Inside the taxi, Grimaldi was drenched in

sweat. One hand drove while his other hand dialed a number on his cellphone.

The blue sedan closed in on him from behind. Grimaldi whipped into oncoming traffic to get away while he desperately waited for someone on the other end of his cellphone to answer.

Sol's cellphone was in vibrate mode on the table alongside the bulletin board in the FBI offices as Grimaldi rang. Sol didn't hear it. He was too busy watching the images from the Vatican.

Back inside the taxi, Grimaldi could only reach Sol's voicemail. Frustrated and terrified, Grimaldi started to leave Sol a message, "This is Father Antonio Grimaldi. I am ..." Grimaldi continued to record his message as he swerved abruptly to miss hitting a slowing car that suddenly stopped in front of him.

He barreled down the highway, deftly dodging oncoming traffic, until he suddenly found himself in the path of an oncoming tractor-trailer.

The taxi's tires screeched and the truck's horn blared as Grimaldi's taxi pancaked hard into the front of the semi and erupted in a ball of flame.

The blue sedan skid to a stop a block behind the inferno. The men inside watched the taxi burn. Satisfied, they drove away.

Inside the White House, the President and the gray-haired man were still glued to CNN.

"It's now officially confirmed," the reporter onscreen announced. "We've just received word that the College of Cardinals has selected a seventeen-year-old boy to be their new Pope!"

The President eyed the gray-haired man confidently as the crowd roared on TV.

In front of the Vatican, the roaring continued as the six hundred thousand strong crowd began cheering and chanting—

Aadam! Aadam! Aadam! Aadam!

A smaller but more unruly crowd outside Aadam's window in Washington was chanting the same as police stopped a few of them from rushing the door to the brownstone eager to get a glimpse of their new Pope. They started screaming wildly as they caught sight of Aadam looking down at them from his window. Aadam started to wave as the news cameras zoomed in on him.

Inside Larson's FBI offices, the staff was riveted to the images of the raucous crowds reacting to Aadam's selection on TV. In the back of the room, Sol finally noticed the voice mail icon flashing on his cell and the visual message:

Missed Call from Father Antonio Grimaldi.
Pissed that he hadn't heard the call, Sol stepped outside into the corridor to evade the commotion and retrieve the voice mail. He input his passcode and his face went numb as the message from Grimaldi began to play. Sol's heart sank as he finished it. His fingers hit the replay button and the last few seconds of Grimaldi's voicemail replayed again on his speaker—"... something is horribly, terribly wrong, Mr. Turner," Grimaldi's urgent message said, "I fear the boy is a—"

Sol couldn't hear the last word of Grimaldi's voicemail. It was drowned out by the massive roar of Grimaldi's taxi imploding as it crashed into the semi.

Sol turned rattled and looked through the glass into the FBI offices where the entire staff was glued to images flashing across the CNN broadcast. The TV was filled with a shot of Aadam waving to the crowd below through the window of his apartment in Washington. As the CNN camera zoomed in further, the entire screen was filled with Aadam's face. Aadam was forcing himself to smile at the crowd, but there was something off about it, the smile was mechanical as was his wave.

A chill ran down Sol's spine as Aadam suddenly looked directly into the camera's lens—directly into Sol's terrified eyes.

Chapter XIII

The White House lawn had a capacity to hold more than a thousand guests. That many and more were gathered to bid farewell to America's shining star. Israel laid claim to the greatest savior on earth for two millennia, yet the country suffered greatly and the notable distinction seemed to do nothing to safeguard Israel's future. As President McCormick stared out over the crowd bidding farewell to Aadam that morning, he was confident that this would bode well for America and its rightful place in history—the birthplace of freedom, the birthplace of a divine messenger of God.

High ranking congressmen and staffers, notable clerics and ministers, dignitaries and the Washington elite all gathered around Aadam saying their goodbyes before Aadam was to depart for Rome to become the new Pope, and more importantly, the world's new hope.

Reporters were interspersed in the crowd and the same CNN announcer who broadcasted from the conclave in the Vatican was on hand at the White House to broadcast the event live to billions of viewers, "... the President will be saying his final good-byes to the young American who, tomorrow morning, will ascend the papal throne at the Vatican. An historic moment for the world for sure, but for the United States, it will mark the first time in history that an American has been elected Pope ..."

Cameras flashed and smiles abounded as the CNN reporter droned on. Everyone seemed euphoric and proud—except for one man brooding in the background. Sol Turner tried to fight the sinking feeling in his gut as he stood there dutifully witnessing what he feared might be the trigger for the downfall of western civilization.

ARMED VATICAN GENDARMES surrounded Aadam as he boarded the chopper winding up on the White House lawn. Sol watched from the base of the boarding ramp as Aadam climbed up it a few feet in front of him. Aadam turned, suddenly realizing Sol was staying behind.

"The Vatican gendarme corps is in charge now. My job's done," Sol told Aadam matter-of-factly.

"I'd like you to come."

"You'll fly in the Vatican's jet to Rome," Sol

replied. "That plane is their sovereign territory, we don't have jurisdiction."

Aadam stood there a moment, sensing something in Sol's eyes. "I don't know what to say. Thank you for everything."

Sol stood there awkwardly before he finally replied, forcing a smile. "Thank you for helping my son."

Aadam nodded and finally walked inside the chopper. Sol left quickly, his fear gnawing away at him.

As the chopper lifted off, Aadam looked down at Sol from the air. Sol never looked back.

NSA STAFFERS WERE working in overdrive that morning. They were monitoring the entire planet for any threat to Aadam's safety. Although the official hand off to Vatican authorities had taken place, until Aadam was safely inside the Vatican, President McCormick felt the United Sates was still the protector of last resort.

An NSA staffer leaned over his monitor eyeing something quizzically. He zoomed in on something on his screen. His face dropped as he grabbed a phone and dialed someone urgently.

In the federal parking lot across from the White House, Simon Novak, the DNI, was climbing into his car after attending Aadam's farewell ceremony. He bumped his head climbing into the driver's seat distracted by his ringing cellphone. He answered irritated. "Yeah. This is Novak."

The NSA staffer was on the other end of the call. He was talking fast and the faster he talked the more Novak's heart raced and his blood pressure climbed. "Aaawww SHIT!" Novak screamed as he slammed his fist onto his dash. "Keep it firewalled till I get there!"

Novak hung up and started the car. He eyed the White House across the street. His plans were hemorrhaging and he had to get to the NSA fast to stop the bleeding.

THE SOUTHBOUND I-95 was congested that morning. Sol didn't mind, the traffic actually allowed him to fumble with his phone and record an audio copy of Grimaldi's voicemail for evidence. Once Grimaldi's voicemail was recorded and transformed to an MP3 file residing safely in his phone's memory, Sol could replay and analyze it. He skipped around, playing bits and pieces of Grimaldi's message to understand the terrifying implications of it—

...the woman felt compelled to reveal the truth and I believe her. She has no reason to

lie...

As he listened to Grimaldi's voice, he knew in his gut the priest was dead and that death was the price Grimaldi paid for the truth he uncovered.

Back inside the NSA, the staffer who called Novak was busy hacking into Sol's AT&T voicemail. He was listening to Sol's voicemail message prompt—

You've reached Sol Turner. Leave a message after the beep.

The NSA tech initiated a password decrypt module on his desktop. Binary code flashed across his monitor as he tried to gain access to Sol's voicemail server.

Meanwhile, as the NSA tech worked feverishly, Sol was still listening to Grimaldi's message—

... I sent the details to the Washington Archdiocese. I regret that decision now as I don't know how high up this goes ...

Inside the NSA, the tech smiled seeing a requester box flash on his monitor—*Password*

Found, it read, *Do you wish to utilize password?* The tech worked the keyboard furiously and suddenly he was stealthily listening to the same voicemail message as Sol. He sat back unnerved hearing Grimaldi's voice.

… something has gone horribly, terribly wrong, Mr. Turner. I fear the boy is—

Then the NSA tech heard the explosion that severed Grimaldi's final, desperate call. The tech worked the keyboard and hit a button to re-play the voicemail. Too late, his face dropped seeing *MESSAGE ERASED* flashing on his screen.

Ninety miles away, Sol hung up from his voicemail. He'd been at this game a long time and knew he had to wipe all his messages from his voicemail server. Could the NSA get them eventually? Sure. But it wasn't as easy as the public thought. Now they'd have to get a FISA warrant over to AT&T to access its backup servers. And that would take time. Not a lot of it but enough for Sol to figure out his next move. Sol was on the run, but so far, at least for now, he was the only one who knew it. Sol activated the Voice Search app on his phone.

"Telephone number and address for—" he

said before stopping abruptly. Sol thought a moment, then quickly disabled the location services on his phone and powered it down.

He swerved to a stop. He looked in every direction, paranoid someone might be following him. He climbed back into his car. Turned on his car's navigation screen. He tapped the *Navigate to Point of Interest* button, then typed in *Archdiocese, Washington, D.C.* Sol's face filled with relief seeing an address appear on the nav screen. He hit the *GO TO* button on his nav and within seconds, the nav unit had routed his new destination. *70 miles away* with a trip time of *one hour and 17 minutes*. Sol piloted the car back onto the road and followed the nav's directions.

NOVAK WAS LIVID. He had finally arrived at NSA and was leaning over the shoulder of the NSA tech who hacked Sol's voicemail. Both were eyeing the audio waveform of the bits and pieces of Grimaldi's voicemail that the tech had managed to download.

"It was the last call Grimaldi made before he died," the tech told Novak. "Turner erased the voice mail before I could harvest the full message."

"I'll have a FISA in an hour to get it off the

backups," Novak replied agitated. "For now, just play back what you got."

The tech pointed to the garbled end of the audio file that represented the last words of Grimaldi's voicemail.

"I had to step-filter the audio," he informed Novak. "The sound of the car exploding drowned out the last word."

"Just *play* it," Novak demanded.

The NSA tech hit a key on his workstation. The audio file played and Novak listened to Grimaldi's voice over the speaker—

... something has gone horribly, terribly wrong, Mr. Turner. I fear the boy is ...

The last word of the audio was still inaudible. Novak glared at the tech.

"Shit, sorry, Sir" the Tech said as he worked the keyboard applying one more denoising filter to the audio file.

"Ok, this should do it." The Tech hit play again and he and Novak leaned in to listen to Grimaldi's final words—

... something has gone horribly, terribly wrong, Mr. Turner. I fear the boy is ... a fake.

Novak's face turned pale.

SOL RACED DOWN the I-95, speeding as much as he could without risking being stopped by the Highway Patrol. A million thoughts slammed into the walls of his brain. His cell rang. He had regretted turning it back on but he didn't want to raise suspicion. He turned location services off but he knew that would just slow down anyone looking for him. Three rings so far and Sol didn't answer. The caller ID was unknown. He finally answered hesitantly, "Hello."

"Sol, it's Simon," Novak replied, calling from the tech's desk inside the NSA.

Novak sounded jovial and upbeat. Sol hung there a moment trying to parse how to handle it. "Hello, Sir. How are you?" he finally replied.

"You skipped out of the ceremony without letting us thank you for doing such a great job with Aadam."

"Well, Sir, it's just that I saw how busy you were with the President."

"Nonsense, Turner" Novak said. "Never too busy for you. Where are you?"

"Ahh ... I'm actually on my way to see my son, Sir," Sol answered nervously.

"Well, when you get done, why don't you

come down? I've got some things to go over with you. And please give Michael my best."

"I'll do that, Sir," Sol replied, forcing himself to stay calm.

"Great," Novak said. "But as soon as you can, okay?"

"Sure will. I won't be long. Goodbye, Sir." Sol hung up rattled. Sol powered downed his phone and swerved off the freeway stopping on an isolated side road. He got out of the car. Looked up paranoid. No choppers. He moved to the trunk and grabbed a tire iron. He swung it and knocked the GPS antenna off his roof.

He climbed back inside the car and smashed the nav unit over and over again until it was just a mangled and empty void in his dash. He went back to the trunk and feverishly pulled off a side panel on the left. He searched the different modules behind the panel. He found the one labeled *Navigation and Sirius Radio*. He used the tire iron to pry it out. He threw it to the ground and smashed it to pieces with the tire iron.

Sol climbed back inside the car. He floored it and barreled away. His antics wouldn't save him, but he knew disabling the car's tracking ability would buy him at least an hour. And that was enough of an edge for someone who knew how to use it.

Inside the NSA, Novak hovered furious over the NSA tech. "What do you mean we had him and now we don't?!"

"We got a positive location ID from the call but his cell just went off line and so did his nav unit," the NSA tech responded nervously.

Novak thought for a moment. "Remote power up his cell and handle it," Novak commanded. Then he stormed out of the room.

Chapter XIV

The offices of the Archdiocese of Washington were housed in an imposing three story stone structure befitting the powerful lobbying arm of the Catholics that it represented. Sol was parked across the street studying its entrance, wondering how he was going to make it inside but, more importantly, wondering how he was going to make it out.

He spotted his answer. A postman with his mail cart. Sol got out of the car with a briefcase. He headed towards the postman and passed in front of him moving up the steps of the Archdiocese's entrance. Before reaching the doors, Sol turned and greeted the mailman who was coming up the steps behind him.

"Hi. Got anything for Archbishop Guilfoyle?" Sol asked the postman cheerfully. "I'm his assistant."

"I'll check," said the postman as he searched a stack of letters and large envelopes. The postman finally came up with a letter and handed it to Sol. "This one's all I got."

"Good enough," Sol replied. "Hey, if you'd like, I'll take it all in for you? Save you some time."

The postman smiled. "That'd be great. I'm running late today. Streets were jammed over this Aadam James thing. Did the kid get down to the Archdiocese? Did you get to meet him?"

"Above our pay grade," Sol answered wryly. "We meet mostly with the sinners down here."

"Well congress is full of them, so you must have a busy schedule!" The two men shared a laugh as the postman handed Sol the stack of mail. Sol nodded his thanks and disappeared inside the Archdiocese's front doors.

While walking through the lobby, Sol sifted through the stack of mail. His heartbeat ratcheted upwards as he found what he was looking for—a handwritten envelope. The sender's name was *Antonio Grimaldi.*

Sol slipped it out of the stack and headed towards the receptionist. She had her back to him filing. Sol put the remaining mail on her desk and slipped out a side corridor.

Once he got back inside his car, he ripped open the envelope and eyed its contents hungrily. Three pages of handwritten notes. He didn't want to linger so he just scanned the contents briefly, the fragments, phrases and scattered glimpses into the secrets that Grimaldi hastily scribbled by hand—

... Carol Hanway believes her sister was the mother of the child ... Her sister disappeared, Carol hasn't seen her in years ... The mother was paid a king's ransom to keep her silence ... When I left Ms. Hanway she was scared ... I don't know how long she'll stay put ... She lives outside Mountville at ...

Shaken by what he read, Sol eyed Carol Hanway's address. He slammed the car in gear and headed out of town towards the freeway.

AFTER A LONG FLIGHT, Aadam's entourage had safely landed and survived the twenty thousand strong crowd that was there to meet them at Rome Fiumicino airport, the hundred thousand cheering onlookers waving at him as his escort weaved through Roman streets and the two hundred thousand strong horde of rapt admirers assembled in front of St. Peter's. Burke was at Aadam's side as they were escorted down Vatican corridors by the Swiss Vatican guard. Aadam seemed strangely calm. Burke seemed on edge. They were met by Cardinal Amato whose greeting was effusive and self-satisfied. Amato was intoxicated with pride. Supposedly, Popes were ordained by the hand of God but, at minimum, Amato had supplied the additional hand.

Aadam looked outside the Vatican windows at the massive crowds assembled outside. For the first time, he was starting to show signs of being overwhelmed by it. Like someone staring into his future. Staring into the abyss.

CAROL HANWAY'S HOUSE was nondescript and unassuming. Probably just the way she wanted it, Sol thought, as he sat in his parked car watching it from a block away.

It was night but there were no lights on inside the house. Sol had waited an hour for her to surface but she was somewhere else. Or perhaps she fled completely hearing of Grimaldi's death.

Sol climbed out if his car and walked to the porch of the house. He eyed the name *Hanway* on the mailbox then he rang the doorbell. Nothing. He eyed the driveway. Empty. It had rained about an hour earlier but there were no signs of tire tracks on the driveway.

Frustrated, he climbed back inside his car and waited.

VATICAN DRESSING ROOMS were notoriously ornate. When Popes were both pontiff and emperor, they were clothed accordingly. The finest fabrics and jewelry, the finest tailors and jewelers, no expense was spared. Aadam remembered Pope Clement's words—w*e saw them as a way to inspire*, he had said of such things. Aadam was troubled by all the opulence and pomposity, and as Amato stood in the background watching the Vatican dresser get Aadam ready, the cardinal grew concerned.

"We had little time but we put our best tailors to the task. Do the vestments meet with your approval?" Amato asked Aadam feigning reverence.

"I understand the historical importance of such things but for me they're unnecessary."

"I know this is all foreign to you but I trust in time you will come to appreciate their purpose." Amato was anxious to change the subject, "and speaking of purpose, Your Holiness, we have many challenges ahead. There is turmoil in God's kingdom, and we have suggestions on how to remedy this."

"The remedy is having the Church submit to God's will," Aadam replied firmly.

"Alas, yes," Amato answered. "But we are tasked with its interpretation."

Aadam was frustrated as the dresser fretted with his robes. He felt like a peacock. He stripped them off.

Amato protested. "But the vestments are traditional, Your Holiness. Crafted to—"

"—crafted to *inspire*. Yes, I realize your intentions but they don't inspire me, nor the Master I serve." Aadam handed the robes to the dresser and stood there in a white linen undergown. "I am ready," he informed Amato.

Amato bristled at Aadam's defiance but he hid it. For now. He bowed and motioned Aadam towards the door. Aadam stepped off the platform and joined the Vatican Swiss guard waiting for him in the corridor.

THE RESTLESS CROWD roared as Aadam finally appeared on the balcony above St. Peters. Seeing his modest clothing, the populist crowd cheered its approval.

A CNN reporter was in their midst and he turned almost giddy to the camera. "Well, he's finally appeared! And the new Pope has rejected the baroque outer garments of his predecessors. He's also rejected a new name. Pope Aadam seems determined to rule as an Everyman and his Church anxiously awaits his new direction!"

NOVAK PACED INSIDE his living room in the wee hours of the morning. He was working the phones, barking orders to the techs at NSA. "Well, keep looking! He's been off-grid ten hours! Where the hell can he be?!"

Inside the NSA, the techs tracking Sol didn't have the answer, at least not one that would satisfy Novak.

"His car's GPS signal has been disabled and his cell is powered off," explained the NSA tech. "He must be using some kind of jailbreak on his phone because we can't trigger a remote power on command. Perhaps he knows, Sir?"

"Or he suspects," Novak replied. "Either way, he's a clear and present danger we can't have floating in the field. Get a locate lock on him and use whatever assets are available to bring him home. I'll authenticate all inter agency approvals."

"Noted, Sir. We're on it." The NSA tech hung up. Novak dialed another number on his cell while the techs at NSA feverishly went to work to find Sol Turner.

SOL DIDN'T SEEM to care. At least it didn't look like it. He had dozed off inside his car, still waiting across the street from Carol Hanway's house. A garbage can sliding across asphalt awakened him. He looked up spotting something. Someone was climbing through the rear window of the Hanway house. He stealthily slipped outside his car and carefully made his way towards the house.

He moved quickly using a hedge as cover and managed to reach the intruder's leg before it disappeared inside the rear window. He yanked on it. The would-be burglar screamed. It was a woman's scream. Carol Hanway's scream.

"What the—?! What the hell are you doing?!" Carol yelled.

"What are you doing?!" Sol countered without letting go of her leg.

"I live here, asshole. Now let go of my leg before I call the cops!"

"I don't think you're interested in calling cops or you'd be using your front door," Sol said as he let her go. "My name is Sol Turner. I'm a friend of Father Grimaldi's. I'd just like to talk to you."

"Grimaldi's dead. It was on the news, in case you hadn't noticed. And I don't want to talk anymore. It's not good for my health. I just came back for some of my things."

"Look, Ms. Hanway, if I found you so can everyone else. I'm a friend. Probably the only chance you got. Talk to me and I'll keep you safe."

Spooked, she studied him. Found something in his eyes that made her feel at ease. "Who are you?" she asked.

Sol whipped out his ID. "Secret Service. The agent in charge of Aadam Samuel James. At least I used to be. Now, I probably should be on the run—just like you."

She studied him another beat. Finally— "You look tired. You like coffee?"

"Doesn't everybody?" Sol answered, forcing a smile.

Carol smiled back. "Ok, I'll make some. Come inside."

"Mind if I use the door?"

She nodded, a bit embarrassed, and climbed back out the window. He followed her towards the front door.

THE VATICAN CARDINALS were assembled again, this time in a cavernous conference room inside the Apostolic Palace. Aadam sat at the head of a massive oval conference table facing the rest of the cardinals seated around him.

Amato was on his feet pacing behind them working his audience. "Our concern is access to credit in world markets. Poorer nations suffer.

Catholics are starved for funds. The International Monetary Fund could use our assistance. If we open our coffers to other banks, we could loan capital. We could provide resources to the poor."

"And just how much is in these *coffers*?" Aadam asked Amato pointedly.

"It's hard to quantify, really. But a substantial amount."

"And where did it come from?" the new Pope replied.

Amato bristled. "Well, prudent investments over the years, of course."

"Investments made from the tithing of the faithful? Donations from the poor?"

"Well, yes. Partially—"

"The very poor that need our help?" Aadam pressed.

"Why, of course but—"

Aadam cut Amato off. "Then why would we *loan* it and not freely *give* it? As it was given to us?"

Cardinal Amato answered, trying hard to cover his irritation. "Because we need our funds to continue God's work."

"Taking care of the poor *is* God's work," Aadam said firmly. "Returning to them that which is theirs *is* God's work."

An older cardinal leaned in unsettled. "Your Holiness, this is not the way things are done. When you've spent more time within these walls, I think you'll—"

"—I think the matter deserves further discussion," Amato interrupted. Amato was anxious to diffuse a debate which was clearly upsetting not only himself but also a host of other cardinals. Cardinals who were happy with a popular Pope who would guide the masses but terrified of one who would guide the fortunes of the Vatican. Fortunes which had been won with centuries of planning, shrewd alliances and blood.

IT WAS ALMOST four in the morning inside Carol Hanway's house. The lights were purposefully dim as Carol sat next to Sol on her sofa. She was beginning to think she could trust Sol but she was terrified of those who might come after him. They sat as two interlopers huddled around a candle, desperate not to be found. Carol nursed a beer while Sol sipped his third cup of coffee spellbound by the story she was telling.

"... the last time my sister Alice called she was in Bali. She was living in a commune. That was seven years ago," Carol recounted.

"Did she talk about her son on that call?"

"No. Nothing about Connor."

Sol raised a brow. "Connor? Is that Aadam's real name?"

"Yep. And that's about all my sister gave him. Birth and a name."

"What about the father? Who was he?" Sol pressed.

"Take your pick," Carol said with a pained smile. "We drank a lot in those days—and drugs, can't say we had an aversion to those either. Hell, my sister was sixteen. I can't blame her for what she did. Connor was a handful."

"Really? How's that?"

"Psycho... Psycho-kin-etics," she replied struggling with the word.

"Psychokinesis?" Sol clarified. "As in, moving objects with the mind?"

"That's it. Sorry, never could pronounce that," she replied. "Yeah, Connor could move stuff. Scared the shit out of Alice. She never wanted a child. She was putting him up for adoption when this guy showed up—"

"What guy?"

"Guy named Brent somethin' or other. He was the head of some fancy *institute*."

"What did he want? Why did he come to see her?"

"He offered to take Connor to a place for special kids."

"And did he?" Sol said, leaning in closer. "Did he take Connor away?"

"After paying Alice a ton of cash and swearing her to secrecy, yes, he took Connor away"

Sol took a moment to process this. His heartbeat was ratcheting higher as he got closer to the truth. "And how long ago was this?"

"Ten years, I guess."

"How old was Connor at the time? Do you remember?"

"Six, maybe. He was just a child."

Sol's mind was racing. "I could really use that man's name. The guy who took Connor away. It's important."

"I think I kept the guy's card somewhere," Carol offered.

"Could you look?" Sol asked, desperate for answers.

She nodded, got up and walked into the other room while Sol was trying to piece everything together. He thought of something and called out to her. "If Connor left when he was six, what makes you so sure that he's Aadam?"

Carol answered as she was searching through the drawers of a chest in her bedroom. "Facial characteristics. That tiny birthmark on his neck. The eyes mainly. Once the eyes of that kid locked into you, you never forget them. Never. Aadam *is* Connor. No doubt about it … Ok, got it!"

Carole emerged from the bedroom holding an old business card in her hand. "Well, I was close on the name, but I suppose for guys in your line of work, close isn't good enough," she said as she handed Sol the card. "Don't know why I kept it all these years. I suppose it reminds me of Connor." She watched Sol as he studied the card. His face was frozen in disbelief. "What's wrong?" she asked.

"Everything," Sol responded. He reread the name of the company on the card—*Advanced Dynamics Institute, Washington D.C.* But it wasn't the company name that made Sol's heart stop; it was the name beneath it, the company's Director of Research—

Arthur Burke

Chapter XV

Inside Aadam's new home, the papal apartment in the Vatican, Cardinal Amato was in the midst of lecturing his young charge. He was finally taking off the gloves

"Countless royals throughout history were thrust into power in their youth, boy-kings in need of mentoring. The smartest among them accepted it, thrived under counsel. You would be well served to follow their example."

Aadam stared at Amato defiantly. "My example lies not in the kingdom of men."

Amato was relentless, clearly rattled by what he perceived as the boy's insolence. "The kingdom of *men* created you, Your *Holiness*. Forget this at your peril."

Amato looked up hearing the door open. Burke walked in. Aadam seemed surprised Burke would take the liberty without knocking.

"I hope I'm not interrupting?" Burke said, feigning propriety.

"Not at all. We were just discussing the direction of the Church," Amato replied.

Burke moved towards Aadam with a calm, assuring smile. "Excellent," Burke replied, placing his hand on Aadam's shoulder.

THE RENT-BY-THE-WEEK apartment Rossen had procured in the outskirts of Richmond was seedy at best, dangerous at worst. Rossen stared numbly at the TV, gun by his side, the bottle of Jack Daniels long since emptied. His eyes were riveted to the newscast on the screen—stock windowed images from the Vatican of Father Grimaldi accompanied by a reporter at the scene of his *accident* outside Lancaster.

"… the Vatican Priest was apparently here on official business and on his way to a small airport outside Lancaster when the driver of his Taxi lost control," the reporter recounted. "They swerved into the oncoming lane and collided with the truck. Both the taxi driver and Father Grimaldi were killed instantly in the crash."

The reporter droned on as Rossen grabbed his cellphone rattled.

ANNE TURNER'S APARTMENT was spotless. She had a cleaning service in a day earlier. She wanted a fresh start. Her son was cured, her husband seemed open to reconciliation and, meeting Aadam, she was filled with hope and happiness. Still, the urgency of the knock at her front door startled her. She eyed her visitor through the peephole. Recognizing a Secret Service agent from her husband's team, she opened it.

"Morning, Mrs. Turner, sorry to disturb you," the agent said with an odd look on his face.

"What's wrong?" Anne said unnerved. "Has something happened to Sol?"

"Honestly, Mrs., Turner, I don't have the answer to that. Which is why I'm here," the agent replied. "Sol's gone missing. Hasn't checked in for 24 hours. He said he was on his way to see Michael but he never showed up at the hospital. We were hoping to find him here."

Anne struggled with the implications of it. "I haven't heard from him since yesterday.

"Well, if you do, please give us a call. This isn't like him. We're a little worried."

"Of course," Anne replied, trying to keep her apprehension in check.

The agent nodded and left. Anne looked after him unsettled.

THE GREYHOUND BUS to North Carolina was almost full. Bus fare was cheaper than rail in rural Pennsylvania and Carol Hanway was also anxious to keep a low profile. A friend of hers had a vacant fifth wheel in Raleigh and Carol figured she'd hide out there until she could come up with a more permanent plan to disappear. She wasn't certain what was in store for her nephew but she was damn sure there was no future in being his aunt.

Sol agreed and before she boarded he handed her what amounted to be nearly half of his cash, three hundred and twenty-three dollars to be exact, to help her on her way. Since the same knowledge had killed, Grimaldi and now had them both on the run, Sol wanted her safe and he wanted distance between them to keep her that way. Sol knew they would come for him. Even if he didn't have all the answers yet, just having the questions would be enough to warrant a bullet in his head. "I'll call you in a few days," he told Carol as she pocketed the money nervously. "If anyone else tries to contact you, don't think, don't linger—just run."

Carol nodded unsettled and disappeared inside the bus. As it drove away, Sol eyed a bookstore in a strip mall across the street. He made his way towards it unsettled.

THREE COMPUTER WORKSTATIONS were nestled behind the Science and Technology section in the rear of the tiny bookstore. Only Sol's workstation was occupied. The others were vacant, costumers used their cellphones for research these days but the anonymity of an internet search on a rent-by-the-hour workstation was the kind of antiquated technology Sol needed to stay a couple of steps ahead of Novak and the NSA. It should buy him a few hours but he worked feverishly just in case.

He was busy scanning the *Duck Duck Go* anonymous search engine results of the three words he typed into its search box: *ADVANCE DYNAMICS INSTITUTE,* the company name that was on Burke's card—the card Carol Hanway said he handed to her sister the day he picked up Connor, the day that presumably began Conner's transformation into Aadam Samuel James. Sol focused on the fragmented search results on his workstation's screen—

ADI breaks new ground in brain research ... ADI awarded funding by the Department of Defense for Psychological Warfare research ... ADI names founding member Arthur Burke as new Director of Operations ...

Fascinated, Sol soaked it all in. His concentration was broken suddenly by a ringing phone. A pay phone near the restrooms. A clerk moved to answer it. Sol jumped up and grabbed the receiver before the clerk could reach it. "It's for me," Sol told the clerk. The clerk eyed him oddly for a moment, then shrugged and walked off.

Sol finally put the receiver to his ear. "Yeah?" he whispered into the line.

LARSON WAS INSIDE his FBI offices on the other end of the call. He was off in a corner looking up every few moments to make sure no one was overhearing their conversation. "They're all over this place looking for you," Larson told Sol. "Anne called. She's freaking out."

"I'll handle it," Sol said agitated. "Did you find anything?"

"Yeah," Larson answered as he flipped back two pages on the notepad in his hands. "When Burke was twenty he was Gottlieb's assistant ..."

"Dr. Carl Gottlieb? At Mk-Ultra?!"

"Yeah, the CIA's mind control program. A

year later, he joined the Stanford Research Institute. That led to the D.O.D. Psychological Warfare grant which he used to fund the startup of the Advanced Dynamics Institute."

"When was this?"

"Ten years ago," Larson answered.

"When Conner disappeared," Sol said out loud, his mind racing.

"Connor? Who the hell is Connor?"

Sol thought hard for a moment before answering. Finally—"I'm expendable now, Frank, and if I let you in, you'll be next on their list. Can you handle that?"

"After twenty years you have to ask, Turner?" Larson bristled. "Now who the hell is Connor?"

"It's Aadam's birth name. Before Burke's people got a hold of him."

"Burke?" replied Larson confused.

"Yeah. Arthur Burke. I saw the business card he handed the kid's birth mother, Frank. Burke raised him. Or programmed him—look, it's muddy. I don't have it all, but I'll get it. But there's not much time. Where's Burke now?"

"Burke's at the Vatican with the kid," Larson answered. He turned paranoid, hearing something outside his office. Nothing. Just a janitor. When he came back on the line, he only heard dial tone.

INSIDE THE BOOKSTORE, Sol was already dialing another number.

Anne jumped up from the couch as she heard a strange ring tone pierce the silence in her apartment. Figuring out the source of the ring-tone that startled her, she raced frantically down the hallway towards a closet next to the kitchen. She swung open the closet doors and reached for a box buried under stacks of kitchen supplies and dinnerware. Odd. The box looked like it had been there for ages. She ripped off the top of it and fished out the circa 2008 Nokia ringing flip phone that was inside it. "Hello!" she said out of breath into the flip phone.

Sol was on the pay phone in the bookstore, relieved that has wife had answered and even more relieved that his safety protocol, the one he set up years earlier, had saved them. At least he hoped it would save them. He spoke in a rushed whisper. "You remember what we talked about? When things go south on us? How we'd handle it?"

Anne was bracing for the worst, but she fought to remain calm. "Yes," she told him.

"Well, this is it."

Her heart sank, hearing those four simple

words from her husband. But if he said them, she knew he meant them and she knew the words must be true. "What happened?! What's—"

"We got thirty seconds," Sol responded, cutting her off. "Wait two days so it looks natural, then take Michael and get out. Make it smart, make it permanent. I will *find you. I promise.*"

Tears welled up in her eyes, her gut wrenched. "But—"

"I love you," he told her softly, "but if we want to live, I have to hang up." Sol started to put down the receiver before he heard her scream—

"Sol wait! Haim Rossen called an hour ago. He said it's urgent. Take this down. He's at 421 555 3605."

Sol hung up. He eyed the second hand ticking away on his watch. The call had taken twenty-nine seconds. He feverishly scribbled the number he had parked in his brain on a notepad. Then he dialed it.

Chapter XVI

THE CHICORY HICKORY truck stop/coffee shop on I-95 outside Richmond had been there since the 60s. Sol thought he remembered eating there once, or maybe he just fueled up his car. His memories were just a blur at that point. He was fighting for his future, his past didn't really matter. Sol was on his third cup of coffee. His nerves were fried. Rossen was late. Sol barely recognized him as Rossen finally slipped through the back door and made his way to Sol's booth in the back. Rossen said nothing as he slipped into the booth across from Sol. But Rossen did notice the .40 caliber cradled stealthily in Sol's lap. Rossen carefully removed the 9mm from his coat pocket and stationed it in his own lap. Sol gave him a subtle nod. They were professionals. They were respectful. And they both knew individually that if they weren't careful they wouldn't survive.

AN HOUR HAD passed. Rossen was on his fourth cup of coffee. Sol hadn't touched his. He was transfixed by Rossen's story. A story told by a man of bullets and blood transformed into a servant of God, a servant terrified by what he had discovered.

"... I never bought the first miracle," Rossen recounted. "That kid run over by the truck—miraculously saved. Two witnesses say the paramedic injected the child that got hit before he recovered. The injection could have been adrenaline. It could have been anything. How would we know? The paramedic is dead."

"You think the paramedic was part of it?" Sol responded nodding. "That the whole thing was premeditated?"

"Definitely. And the fire in the nursing home. Witnesses said Aadam's skin *glistened* as the fire raged. They admitted he was standing in the hallway where the sprinkler system was *working* before he went into the burning room. I say they preloaded the plumbing with water and Zel gel …"

"The stuff stunt men coat themselves with before they film a fire stunt …" Sol said, his mind racing.

"Precisely. Or its equivalent. Any kind of glycerin retardant like that would have given him immunity to the flames."

Rossen was convincing. The pieces of the

puzzle, or more accurately, the twisted conspiracy were finally coming together inside Sol's brain. "And what about the other miracles?"

"A crop duster flew over the church the morning of the assault," Rossen said, pulling out a picture of a biplane flying over the church. "This was taken an hour before the siege. It would explain why it rained over the church and nowhere else."

This hit Sol hard. "Cloud seeding …"

"You got it," Rossen answered. "The Chinese have done it for years. Hardly miraculous if your resources are infinite."

"Governmental complicity—"

"And a desperate need for a savior," Rossen replied. "You have a world splitting apart at the seams, so create a false god to sew it back together again. Nothing new. Mankind has been doing this for millennia."

Sol was reeling. Disgusted. Defeated. Shamed he had played a part in the plan. "And you told your superiors all this?"

"Yes," Rossen replied, his face filled with disgust.

"Then why? Why would they go along with it? Why would they be complicit?"

Rossen smiled at Sol's naiveté. "We are Jews, Turner. We are pragmatists. Not out of conscience but out of necessity."

"So better a Christian messiah than a Wah-habi sheikh …"

Rossen nodded reluctantly.

"So you're just going to sit back and let this happen?" Sol said frustrated.

"Do I have a choice? Grimaldi's dead. How long do I have?" Rossen suddenly alerted to something outside in the parking lot. A man climbing out of a white van in the distance.

Rossen turned to Sol angrily, "You were followed!"

Sol turned, spotting the van. "No. Not one of mine." Sol slapped down a twenty and they quickly emptied the booth slipping out a side door.

They moved rapidly towards the opposite end of the parking lot where Sol and Rossen ran smack into four armed men exiting another van. Sol and Rossen whipped out their guns but it was over in a millisecond as a bullet from a silenced .45 punctured Rossen's forehead. At that same moment, Sol's body went limp, the tentacles of a Taser gun piercing his back.

The four men stealthily picked up Sol and shoved him into the back of a van. They pulled Rossen's body off the pavement and pushed it into a culvert. Then they climbed inside the van and it sped away.

The entire assault took less than 45 seconds. No witnesses. Not that the assailants cared. In their minds, they were fighting to save the world. And whoever had to be sacrificed for the cause was just collateral damage. Sol Turner would have the option Rossen wasn't offered. A second chance. On levels he might never even fathom.

Chapter XVII

The turbines of the DC-10 sucked air as it banked snapping Sol back to consciousness. His eyes struggled to focus. He'd been drugged. He found himself bound and gagged in the cargo hold of an airplane. Destination unknown.

A dark featured man moved towards him with a syringe. Sol groaned as it punctured his thigh. As the second dose kicked in, Sol's eyes fluttered.

A BLACK MERCEDES wove through the crowded streets of Mardan in northern Pakistan. Sol was in the back seat of the car, confused and still drowsy. He was flanked by two large bearded Arabs. They sandwiched him in with their bodies. Sol eyed the sea of impoverished humanity streaking past him out the window. He was in no shape to make an escape. And even if he was, Mardan was not famous for offering sanctuary to Americans seeking refuge. He'd be lucky if he lasted five minutes out there. So he was content to stay in the car. He was sure things would change at the end of his journey. Wherever that was, contentment there would surely elude him.

THEY DRAGGED SOL down a long corridor in a large warehouse in the outskirts of Mardan. He didn't resist, the Arabs dragging him were taller, stronger and heavily armed. Sol was being kept alive for a reason so he figured now wasn't the time to complicate matters with resistance.

Two more Arab guards opened a door at the end of the corridor and the other men dragging Sol pulled him into a dark, cavernous room. Sol could smell fish. Though empty now, it must have been some kind of a packing warehouse. This observation would only have relevance if Sol ever had to find the place again. Right now, he only gave himself a 50/50 chance of making it out of there alive, so he ignored the smell of fish and focused on the door that just opened on the opposite side of the room and the four men who ushered in a bearded sheikh that was all too familiar to him.

Sol had been tracking Sheikh Ansari for years. He had threatened the assassination of the President along with the Vice President and Secretary of State. Ansari's men were most surely responsible for the terrorist assault on the church, the assassination attempt outside the holding facility and God knows what else. Sol's eyes were searching for the closest weapon he could lunge for. If he was going to die in there, Sol would do everything in his power to make sure Ansari died with him.

Sol was forced into a chair and then bound to it by heavy rope. A chair was placed across from him and Sheikh Ansari sat down slowly on top of it. Ansari didn't speak at first; instead, the man at his side did the greeting. Sol recognized him immediately. It was Hassan Nassif, the Muslim *postulator* who questioned Aadam with Rabbi Rossen and Father Grimaldi.

"I hope your trip was pleasant, Mr. Turner?" Nassif said as he hovered behind Ansari.

"What am I doing here?" Sol asked, glaring at him.

"Testing your faith. I trust you'll do better than they did." Nassif shined a flashlight on two dead bodies propped up against the walls across the room—the two CIA agents Larson called in Lahore. Their faces were bloody from the loss of their tongues.

Sheikh Ansari studied the horror and outrage on Sol's face before he finally spoke.

"Next time send someone competent to try

and kill me. Or at least have the decency to try yourself," Ansari said calmly.

Sol lunged at him, jerking himself upwards. The Arab guards slapped him down and held his chair to the floor. They were going to start beating him, Ansari waved at them to stop.

"Mr. Turner, as you may have guessed, I am Sheikh Tariq Ansari. You've burned a lot of resources looking for me."

"Apparently not enough," Sol said icily.

"Well, now we've found each other."

"So we have. So why am I still alive?"

"Because you are close to the boy," Ansari answered.

"The boy you're trying to kill."

"Kill?" Ansari replied, shaking his head incredulously. "We were trying to *save* him."

Sol eyed Ansari venomously. "Oh, right. That's why you sent a team of assassins to the church."

"They were sent to keep him from harm."

"Along with the innocents who died that day?! Twelve murdered, three of them children!"

"An unfortunate outcome," said Ansari. "Our motives were pure."

"The same motives of your rooftop assassin outside our holding facility?!"

Ansari eyed him confused. "He was not ours."

"Sure," Sol answered, tilting his head back disgusted. "And neither was the pilot who hijacked our transport?"

"Again, we were attempting to capture the child. Save him from—"

"Oh, let's just cut the bullshit, okay Sheikh?!" Sol yelled. "I've been drugged, beaten—I'm fucking tired! Save the boy from *what?!*"

"His destiny," Ansari answered.

Sol eyed him thrown as Ansari continued.

"Three years ago I had a vision that the Mahdi, or *Messiah* in your parlance, would come. He would perform miracles. He would be embraced by all and he would ascend to power."

"So you fear the end of Islam?"

"*NO*. The opposite!" Ansari argued. "He has the potential to *unify* us all with his guidance, the living word. One world, reconciled under a common God speaking with a common voice. A voice of the present, verifiable, documented concurrently instead of centuries later."

"I'm not getting this, Sheikh," Sol said combatively. "If he's your savior, why does he have to be *saved*?"

"Because his death will be used as a pretext

for war and the theft of resources."

"His death?" Sol said, rolling his eyes. "The kid's 17. He'll outlive us all!"

"The child will not live out the week," Ansari warned. "They are planning to martyr him."

"What?!" Sol said incredulous.

Ansari leaned in. "A Judas walks among them. I saw all this in my vision. A man of dark skin will kill the child and the world shall weep while those responsible extract their vengeance on those who had nothing to do with it."

Sol's brain was spinning. Given what he learned from Grimaldi and Rossen, he knew there were forces aligned to exploit the kid. But murdering him was not on Sol's radar and the visions of radical sheikhs weren't the kind of intel high on his reliability list. Still, Sol decided to play along. "Look, if you believe this, why tell me?"

"Because we have done all we can," the sheikh answered. "You've destroyed most of my network. Killed most of my men. I lack the ability to get close to him. An ability held only by you."

"Me? How?"

"He trusts you. You can get near him. We can arrange this."

"And then what?"

"You can warn him. You can save him."

Sol took a long beat before answering. "And if I think you're wrong about this assassination? If I think Aadam isn't your *Messiah* or your *Mahdi* but I think he's a fake or something even worse? What then?"

Ansari got up and moved over to Sol. The sheikh's eyes were filled with a fearful desperation.

"Then the boy who saved your son's life will die by your negligence."

Sol just sat there, torn, shaken. Ansari signaled his men to untie him. As they released his bindings, Sol eyed Ansari confused.

"Help us or leave, Mr. Turner. The choice is completely yours."

"You'll just let me walk out of here?"

"Yes."

"Without shooting me in the back?"

"If I wanted you shot it would have happened outside that coffee shop with the Shin Bet agent. I would not have expended the resources to fly you across the Atlantic."

Ansari motioned to his men. The guards blocking the door parted. They opened the door showing Sol the empty, unguarded corridor beyond them. Sol shook his head and headed towards the door. He was almost out of it and into the empty corridor behind it to freedom before he stopped. He really didn't know what triggered it. Certainly not his survival instincts or his self-interest. Maybe it was that fleeting memory of his son telling him he was cured while he stood overwhelmed on the stage with Keisha. Or maybe it was something bigger than that, something unknown to him but something whose power didn't come from the known. Whatever it was, it made him turn back to face the sheikh—

"What do you want me to do?"

THE BLACK MERCEDES rolled to a stop on a crowded street in Mardan. A body was tossed out its rear doors and the car sped away.

The body rolled and came to a stop on the road. It was bruised and battered. It was Sol Turner. A crowd of Pakistani peasants rushed to his aide. They helped him to his feet. Sol's haggard eyes stared at the U.S. flag waving above the American embassy a block away from him. Sol limped towards it.

A NURSE WAS busy dressing Sol's wounds inside the embassy as the U.S. Ambassador to Pakistan entered holding a secure portable Sat phone. The Ambassador waved the nurse outside and handed the phone to Sol.

"Yes, sir," Sol said into the phone, knowing who was on the other end of it.

Novak was in his office. The Director of National Intelligence looked almost as haggard as Sol. He'd been up all night, ever since he got word that Sol had surfaced. "You had us worried," Novak told him. "I heard Ansari's men roughed you up pretty bad?"

"They grabbed me on my way home from the White House. I never saw it coming."

"Ok, not too much over the phone," Novak cautioned. "We'll debrief you on the flight home."

"No! There's no time, Sir," Sol insisted. "Before I escaped, I overheard their plans to kidnap the boy."

"Kidnap? Aadam? When?"

"Two days, Sir. Ansari plans to hold him for ransom and kill him if he doesn't get it. I need to get over there. I need to make sure his security is tight. I saw faces around Ansari. I can ID them and tell our guys who to look out for."

Novak was broadsided by this. He thought about it hard before answering.

"Okay," Novak finally said. "You can brief our escort team on the way. I'll arrange transport."

AN HOUR LATER, Arthur Burke was inside a Vatican office on the phone with Novak.

"... it's problematic, him coming here. Aadam's been asking for him. I've said Turner's been busy on other assignments."

Still in his office, Novak answered Burke firmly. "Intel's Ansari intercepts confirm what Turner's saying. We don't want our plans compromised by the actions of others. Tell me you understand this?"

Burke thought a moment. Began warming to the change of plans. "Of course I understand. And actually there's a possibility Ansari and the nuisance he's causing us can be used to our advantage."

"I've thought of that too," Novak replied. "We must never let a good crisis go to waste. Insulate Turner. Find out all he knows."

"Count on it," Burke said before hanging up the phone. Burke took a moment to watch a gardener tending to roses in the Vatican grounds outside before turning to Cardinal Amato, who was waiting impatiently hovering over his desk across from him.

"Well?" Amato asked nervously. "Are we okay?"

"We're fine, Cardinal. We'll just be adding another *miracle* to your mix. The more the better, I should think."

The cardinal eyed him quizzically as Burke grabbed the phone and dialed another number.

Chapter XVIII

A Citation X jet landed on runway 34C at Rome Fiumicino airport. As it taxied to a stop, Sol stared out the window wondering what future was in store for him. The two Secret Service agents escorting him to the Vatican opened the side door to the fuselage. Sol followed them down the ramp to the runway where they were met by two members of the Vatican gendarme corps. One of the Secret Service agents spoke quietly to one of the gendarmes. "He's all yours," the Secret Service agent said, "and he's clean."

Sol couldn't hear what they were saying but he knew he was being handed over to the Vatican's *care*. He wasn't handcuffed physically but if his moves signaled any kind of threat, he was certain the gendarmes were authorized to neutralize that threat. Most likely with extreme prejudice.

ROME FIUMICINO was usually the most heavily trafficked airport in Europe. That day was no exception. Sol and his Vatican escort snaked through the crowded terminal towards the parking lots outside. Sol was searching for something in the aisles. He spotted it. The men's restroom sign. He turned to one of the gendarmes. "Sorry, but I need to make a pit stop. I overdid the Evian on the way over."

Expressionless, the gendarme nodded.

"Thanks, you're a prince," Sol said as he headed into the restroom.

There were five stalls and three urinals. Two patrons were heading out, leaving only a small boy washing his hands assisted by his father. The *father* had a familiar face and Sol knew it well. He was one of Ansari's bodyguards. He was clean-shaven now and dressed in a fashionable Italian suit. He nodded subtly to Sol then exited the restroom with the boy.

The gendarmes spotted the man with the boy leaving the restroom and watched him closely. Not because he aroused suspicion but because he was greeted by a beautiful blonde. The gendarmes watched the *family* disappear uneventfully into the crowd.

Meanwhile, Sol was in the last stall in the restroom. He reached up behind the toilet and retrieved what Ansari's bodyguard left for him. He unwrapped the sub compact Kahr 9mm that was bundled with a tiny digital tape recorder. He quickly strapped the recorder under his shirt and shoved the Kahr PM9 in the small of his back.

Sol left the restroom and rejoined the gendarmes without fanfare. They headed towards the exits, passing a video monitor alive with a CNN International broadcast. Images of Chinese riots in Beijing flashed across the screen accompanied by the CNN commentator's voice over—

"... More violence erupted in China as citizens react to the increase in commodity prices and the erosion of their currency since it was finally forced to decouple from the dollar," the CNN commentator noted. "The net worth of Chinese citizenry is plummeting and the usually ironfisted government in Beijing is having a difficult time keeping control ..."

Sol got a fleeting glimpse of the CNN images before he was whisked outside. He wondered how bad things would get and how they planned to use Aadam to *fix* it.

MORE VIOLENT IMAGES flashed across another monitor. This one was inside Cardinal Amato's office. The images were of protesters clashing with police outside a baroque building in downtown Rome. Burke and Amato watched the broadcast with interest. As they listened to a CNN commentator describe the conflict, they seemed encouraged by the melee.

"... Thousands descended on Rome today as the G20 begins meeting to address the global economic meltdown," the CNN reporter explained. "The Vatican has pledged its support and for the first time in history, a sitting Pope, Pope Aadam James, will take part in the economic summit ..."

Burke turned as Amato's aide poked his head inside. "They're here, Eminence," said the aide. Amato nodded and Sol was escorted inside by the gendarmes.

THE DEBRIEFING WENT better than Sol expected. Burke was skeptical but Sol knew that whatever sick, sinister use Burke had for Aadam, the plan had been in place for years and Burke couldn't afford to dismiss Sol's dire and emphatic warning. "... Ansari's assault may be imminent," Sol continued to explain. "You've got to keep him sequestered in the Vatican:"

"That's impossible" Amato replied. "He needs to be visible, *seen,* to inspire confidence—"

"—He can't inspire anyone if he's dead!" Sol countered agitated.

Burke studied Sol for a moment. Sol looked emaciated, malnourished and on edge.

"How did you learn of Ansari's plans?" Burke asked him.

"Trust me, it wasn't a conscious effort on my part," Sol answered. "I heard his men in the background while they tortured me."

"If they took the trouble to torture you, they expected something in return. What do you think they were after?"

"I guess they figured I knew the most about Aadam's security. They probably wanted to be sure they didn't miss something, something that could foil their plan."

"And did you provide that *something*?"

"What are you inferring, Burke?" Sol bristled.

"Did you *tell* them anything?"

Sol got right in Burke's face. "I told them *nothing*. Look, this isn't about me, it's about Aadam. And just what the hell are you doing here, anyway, Burke? I never took you for a religious man."

Sol's indignation became a convincer for his sincerity in Burke's mind. Burke was anxious to deescalate. "I'm here to minister to Aadam's psychological needs."

Sol smiled cynically. "Right. Okay, look,

gentlemen, you've had your time here but Aadam's is running out. Where is he? I want to talk to him. That's why I'm here."

"He's very busy, I'm afraid," Amato blurted out. "He can't really be interrupted. He—"

"Sol?"

Sol spun around to see who was calling his name. It was Aadam. The *Pope* was standing at Amato's door. "I heard you were here," Aadam said, concerned, but happy to see him. "Are you alright?"

Sol walked over to him. "No worries, I'm fine," Sol assured him. "But I'd like a word with you."

"Of course," Aadam replied.

Sol started to leave with him and Burke quickly followed. Sol turned back to Burke abruptly and glared at him. "Look, I'm in the escort business, not you. Do you mind?"

Burke eyed Aadam.

"It's okay. He's my friend," Aadam told him. Burke nodded reluctantly allowing Sol and Aadam to leave by themselves. After they disappeared down the corridor, Burke eyed Amato unsettled.

AADAM SEEMED STRANGELY at peace as he walked with Sol through the lush, heavily manicured Vatican gardens outside the Papal Palace. The two gendarmes followed, but they allowed Sol and Aadam their space. Sol kept an eye on them as he tried to convince Aadam of the seemingly inconvincible. "… What I'm saying is that you're not *safe* here!" he told the boy urgently.

"I'm not concerned," Aadam replied calmly.

"Well, you should be," Sol said firmly as he eyed the gendarmes getting closer to them. Sol spotted a large granite crypt a few yards away. He motioned Aadam over to it. Before the gendarmes could stop them, Sol and Aadam moved inside the crypt where Sol locked the metal door behind them. They wouldn't have much time; the gendarmes were already knocking on the metal doors. Sol grabbed Aadam by the shoulder and locked eyes with him.

"How long have you known Arthur Burke?"

"Not long. You introduced me to him."

Sol searched Aadam's eyes. They were genuine. "No memory of meeting him previously?"

"None," Aadam replied firmly.

The gendarmes were pounding on the door now. Sol knew he only had seconds.

"Look, I am in your debt. You're a talented kid, wise beyond your years—but you're *no* Messiah."

"I am a messenger of the Lord."

"Cut the bullshit!" Sol yelled. "Everyone's buying it *but not me*. You've been brainwashed. Understand?! Part of a covert program. Everything you've done, every single miracle has been staged! You may believe it, everyone else may believe it, but it doesn't make it real! It's a myth! And before anyone can prove it, they will kill you to keep the myth alive! Do you understand what I'm telling you, Aadam? They are going to *martyr* you!"

Aadam just eyed Sol numbly. The words had clearly shaken him, and they obviously had a deep, inexplicable resonance because Aadam was struggling with everything inside him to stay calm.

He finally started to speak before gasping as—*Thwapp*! Something knifed through the air and pierced the skin on Sol's neck. As Sol fell limp to the ground, Aadam looked out the crypt's tiny window and spotted the sniper on the roof of the Apostolic Palace two hundred yards away.

Sol started to lose consciousness on the floor of the crypt. As he did, he finally noticed the tiny, clandestine video camera watching them from the corner of the ceiling. Its red LED activity light flickered as if it was winking at him,

mocking him for thinking that he could somehow foil a plan decades in the making.

Chapter XIX

Deep beneath the Vatican in an ancient cell hewed out of limestone and dripping with moisture, Burke hovered over Sol who was strapped to a chair and groggy. The etorphine-laced dart shot from the sniper's tranquilizer gun was fast acting and slow to wear off. Sol would feel its partial numbing effects for days. If he lived that long. Burke would do his best to see that he wouldn't.

There was a small monitor on a table in front of Sol. Burke triggered the playback of video surveillance footage from the camera inside of the crypt where Sol took Aadam. The audio was captured by a long-range parabolic mic. It was scratchy, but audible. *Do you understand what I'm telling you, Aadam? They are going to martyr you!* the tape replayed. Burke stopped the playback and held up the Kahr PM9 and tiny recording device Sol retrieved from the bathroom.

"Aadam's convinced you meant to do him harm," Burke said smugly before he struck Sol in the side of the face with the butt of the gun.

"What do you know about us, Turner?"

Sol winced from the pain but he wasn't going to give Burke the satisfaction of seeing him break. "I only know what I told you. I was just trying to warn him about Ansari."

Burke hit him hard in the face a second time. The look on Burke's face was rabid. He was finally free to reveal himself and the inner rage that fueled him.

"We know Grimaldi left you a voice mail. He sent a letter to the Archdiocese. You intercepted it. Their cameras taped you in the lobby. What was in it, Turner?"

Sol glared at Burke giving him nothing. Burke hit him again. Harder. Sol almost passed out. Burke watched impassively.

"You have a chance to save your wife and son. Just tell me what you know."

"They have nothing to do with this!"

"They do now," Burke replied menacingly.

"Careful, asshole. You go there and you, everyone you know, everyone close to you are dead, trust me on that," Sol said icily.

Burke slammed him hard again. "It's the other way around, Turner."

Sol fought to stay conscious. Decided to go for broke. *Screw it*, he thought, *I'll die here anyway*. So he went for it, hoping Burke's ego was the Leviathan he thought it was.

"Tell me about the program, Arthur. Your baby, right? A great gimmick but seriously, Doc, how long you think he can pass as the impostor *Messiah* that he is?"

"Hopefully two millennia like the first one," Burke responded wryly.

Sol kept playing. "The miracles were nice. How'd you do it? The downpour on the church, cloud seeding, I got that. Fire gel for the burn rescue in the nursing home, adrenaline shot for the kid injured in the hit and run, but the sniper—that one eludes me, how'd you do that?"

Burke was impressed enough with Sol's appreciation of the genius of his plan that he stopped hitting him. "Haines was invaluable but he knew too much," Burke revealed. "The sniper's bullet that killed him was real. Aadam's bullet was made of Teflon, strategically targeted to pierce him without damage."

"So, the sniper was yours."

"Yes."

"And the cops who killed him?" Sol said, knowing the answer.

"Ours too. Unlimited resources. Unlimited miracles."

"And my son. How'd you do that one?"

Burke smiled at Turner, content to tell him

the truth that would break Sol's heart.

"Michael was the simplest. His disease was purposely misdiagnosed. It was a bacteriological warfare virus we've been testing. We just needed to wait for the right time to inject him with the antidote."

"When Aadam was present. ..." Sol said, reeling.

"Yes."

Sol's torment was building, "So you waited until you could make it a media event—on *Keisha*—you let my son suffer! You sick, sadistic son of a bitch, you'll die for this!"

Sol tried to jerk himself out of the chair, his face bulging with rage. Burke beat him back and continued beating him savagely punctuating the vicious blows while screaming—*"TELL ME WHAT YOU KNOW, TURNER!"*

"Enough!" yelled a voice from the doorway of the cell. Burke turned as a tall, well-dressed gray-haired man entered the room. He was the man who visited the President at the White House, the man pulling the strings from the shadows, the man who was clearly Burke's superior in all this.

Burke backed off as the gray-haired man moved calmly to Sol.

"This is bigger than you and your son, Mr.

Turner," the gray-haired man said. "It's about humanity. Its chances for survival."

Sol looked up groggily. The man's face was familiar. But Sol couldn't place him; his mind was more focused on staying conscious, conscious enough to find a way out.

"I don't believe I've had the pleasure, Mr. ?"

The gray-haired man didn't feel the need for an introduction, he just continued his lecture, "America as an idea was promising but it's over, Mr. Turner. The world's lost confidence in us. It's splitting apart at the seams. It needs order; I dare say *direction* from the divine."

"How the hell does that bring order?" Sol replied angrily. "No one cares about the Pope."

"They care when he's the *second* son," said the gray-haired man. "And they definitely care about his money."

The full gestalt. And Sol was finally able to wrap his head around it. "... The resources of the Vatican ..." Sol said, whispering his thoughts out loud.

The gray-haired man smiled while he nodded. "Trillions before you leverage the real estate. And with this newfound Messianic fervor, a tithing, tax payer base that's unprecedented."

"… With more than enough to become the world's leading banker ... surrogate for the fallen in London and New York ..." Sol said numbly.

"Precisely. There art no greater loyalty than the faithful's to a generous God."

Sol stared at him defiantly. "So you think you can martyr him before he makes trouble? You're insane. It'll never work."

"Sure it will," the gray-haired man said smugly. The Church ruled a millennium in the name of a prophet whose miracles were evangelized by third party witnesses. Hell, ours are documented on hi-def video, alive and viral on You Tube. Aadam is bulletproof."

"Except for the one that kills him."

"It worked handsomely for his predecessor," the gray-haired man said smiling.

If Sol's hands weren't bound, he would have ripped both their heads off their bodies and mounted them on a stick in front of the Vatican. But Sol's hands weren't free, so he had to resort to words.

"So who are you going to use? A Muslim assassin?"

"A Muslim *fanatic*. Then we'll crush the fundamentalists worldwide for revenge and our young martyr will leave behind a new gospel inclusive of all."

"*All* who submit to your will," Sol replied icily.

"*God's* will," the gray-haired man said reverently.

"You don't believe in God any more than I do," Sol said before turning away disgusted.

The gray-haired man smiled. But he was finished there. He headed outside with Burke.

The guards in the corridor locked the doors to Sol's cell while the gray-haired man huddled with Burke.

"Give me time. I can break him," Burke said.

"No need to break him. His family will provide the incentive. Are we on schedule?"

Burke checked his watched and nodded. "He just landed," Burke told him confidently.

AN ALFA ROMEO Giulia was driven to a Hertz rental kiosk in the parking lot of the Milan Airport. The Hertz lot driver got out and handed the keys to the man who would be renting it. The customer was a dark featured Arab man who thanked the driver and placed his only luggage, a long, dark green duffel bag, in the rear seat before he climbed inside. He pressed the ignition button, fastened his seat belt and waited for the nav screen to boot up. Once it did, he entered his destination:

12 Via di San Sebastianello, Rome

Chapter XX

Anne was packing feverishly inside her bedroom. She would have to leave almost everything behind, whatever didn't fit into her car and she didn't even know the reason why. But when that phone went off in her closet, the ring alone told her life, as she knew it, was over. And for Michael too. He was alongside her helping her shove clothing into one of four suitcases when they both heard the knock at the door. Anne looked at her watch. 11 p.m. Odd. She moved carefully to the hallway and headed towards the front door. She inched next to it looking out the peep hole when—

Bammmm! The front door crashed inwards. Anne and Michael screamed as a large man grabbed her, pressing gauze over her face. She collapsed lifeless on the floor.

TWO VATICAN GENDARMES opened Sol's cell door. Sol readied himself for another beating. But it didn't come. Instead, one gendarme took out an Mp3 player. Sol heard Anne and Michael screaming during the fight with the man who breached their front door.

"My son just got out of the hospital!" Sol yelled coiled in shock. "He's sick!"

"All the more reason to cooperate," one of the Vatican gendarmes told him callously.

The other gendarme trained a gun on Sol while his partner pulled out a set of handcuffs and moved towards their captive. As he reached for Sol's hands, Sol erupted in rage. He lunged at the cuffs, twisting them from the gendarme's grip and wrapped them around the gendarme's neck putting the guard in the other's line of fire.

Fueled by a jackhammer rush of adrenaline, Sol shoved his captive forward, driving him into the other gendarme with the gun. Both bodies crashed into the cell door.

Sol wrapped the cuffs around his fist. He savagely beat the face of the one guard while kicking the other in the stomach.

The first fell unconscious, his jaw broken and bloody. Sol turned his attention to the second who was too battered to repel Sol's Rottweiler blows to his face. In seconds, it was over.

Sol gasped for breath. No time to linger. He listened for anyone coming. Nothing. He grabbed the guards' guns and radios.

THE VATICAN SECURITY office was at the top of the narrow stairs ascending from the basement. Sol moved up that staircase slowly, careful to blend in. The Vatican gendarme uniform from one of the guards he subdued would help with that, but his battered face might give him away. Luckily, the single guard in the Vatican security office was busy watching a CNN international broadcast on one of his many monitors.

The images onscreen were of crowded Roman streets where protesters were waiving anti-G20 signs. The audio blared as a CNN commentator reported from the scene—

"... This will be the Pope's first public appearance as the papal procession winds its way to the G20 summit held this year in the historic buildings surrounding the Piazza Navona ..."

Sol was just a yard behind the guard in the security office before the gendarme finally sensed him and turned. The gendarme smiled at first seeing Sol's uniform. The smile disappeared when the guard's eyes focused on Sol's bloodied face. By then it was too late. Sol was already on top of him. It was over fast, he smashed the gendarme's head into his desk four times before the guard slumped unconscious in his chair. Sol grabbed the gendarme's cellphone and started dialing.

ON A HIGHWAY outside of Rome, the Arab man who rented the Alpha was driving leisurely towards an exit sign reading *Roma—Vaticano*, a kilometer ahead of him.

The man was savoring his time in the shiny new Giulia. He had always wanted to drive one. He requested the perk at the last minute. The people who hired him granted it after a few minutes of arguing back and forth about the extravagance. The man won them over. After all, the parties involved intuitively knew this would probably be the last car he would ever drive. So they let him choose it and paid the 500 euro daily fee to rent it. Twenty minutes after he would take the exit ahead of him, the rental period would technically terminate. The man didn't know who would retrieve the car after he would abandon it—and he didn't really care. He got his five hours in behind the wheel and, to his surprise, he wasn't impressed. The steering was rather tenuous and he was a man preoccupied with how things handled. The scoped sniper rifle disassembled in his duffel bag met his strict standards in that regard. The Alpha Giulia did not.

THE STREETS OUTSIDE the Vatican were clotted with a crowd of at least three hundred thousand onlookers all hoping for an *up close and personal* experience with their new Pope. Still in the gendarme uniform, Sol wove his way stealthily through the crowd talking to Larson using the cellphone he took off the guard in the security office.

"... I don't have details, Frank," he told Larson urgently. "I just know it's today."

Larson was in the far corner of his FBI office in Washington speaking in hushed tones to Sol over his cell. He was careful not to let anyone hear him.

"They say you've gone rogue, Sol," Larson said nervously. "They say you took out three guards."

"Look, there's no time for this, Frank!" Sol replied angrily. "They've got Anne and they've got Michael. Send a team to her apartment. There'll be signs of a struggle. You've got to trust me on this!"

Larson weighed it a long beat. "Alright, alright. Calm down," he finally said. "What are you gonna do?"

"Who's in charge of the kid's security?" Sol asked urgently.

"Rawlins."

Sol considered it a moment. "Rawlins is a good man. There's no way he can be in on this. Call him, Frank."

"And tell him what?"

"What I've told you. Tell him everything. Tell him that I'll be contacting him. You gotta do it, Frank. If you don't, the kid dies and it'll be on your head." Sol looked up seeing a phalanx of police coming towards him. "I gotta go. Just do it, I beg you! I'll be in touch."

Sol hung up. He took the battery out of the cellphone and smashed it under his foot before he slipped unseen into the crowd.

TRACKING THE CALL took less than sixty seconds. Still, Larson hovered over his FBI tech impatiently waiting for the locate. The tech worked the keyboard at his workstation and finally looked up victorious.

"You got him?" Larson said, leaning in for a look.

The tech nodded. "Turner called from a cellphone registered to Giuseppe Rollo, a Vatican gendarme."

"Where?"

The tech pointed at coordinates on his mapping software. "The cell tower transmitting his signal was here so Turner's got to be within a two mile radius outside St. Peter's."

Larson looked up frustrated, "Shit, Henderson, Turner *gave* us that much. Keep monitoring until you've got precise coordinates."

Larson turned agitated to another agent. "Get over to Anne Turner's apartment. Turner says someone grabbed her and his son."

The agent nodded and hurriedly left the office as Larson's mind raced. Larson knew Sol was solid, but the story Sol told him shook him to his core. If it was false and he acted on it, his career was over and he'd be looking at ten to thirty without parole. If the story was true and he didn't act, history wouldn't be kind to him; history wouldn't be kind to anyone.

Chapter XXI

SEAN RAWLINS WAS built like a nose tackle. His 6'4" African American frame squeezed out of his Secret Service Suburban on the streets outside the Vatican as he was filled in by Larson over his cellphone.

"Who else is in the loop on this?" Rawlins asked, still trying to wrap his head around what Larson told him. Rawlins' job was to protect the Pope. Officially, Turner was just uprated to an imminent threat, but he knew Turner and he didn't buy Turner going rogue.

"You're the only one so far," Larson told him. "If Turner's telling the truth, we won't know who to trust. My team's at his wife's place. He wasn't lying. There were signs of a struggle and she and his son are missing."

"Turner trained me, Frank. Recommended me for two bumps in rank. I'm down for him."

"Then what's the plan?" Larson asked. "According to Turner we don't have much time."

"We go with it," Rawlins replied. "Taking him at his word is consistent with protecting the kid so we have nothing to lose. I'll brace my guys. You work it from your end"

Larson was relieved Rawlins was onboard. "I've got agents at the embassy. I'll send them over."

"We'll need them. Keep me posted. I'll be checking in."

Rawlins hung up and waved over three of his Secret Service team. They huddled together while Rawlins laid out the possible threat. "There's chatter about an assassination attempt today," he told them. "No confirmation. Just giving you the heads up."

The other agents eyed him nervously, especially a young white agent with a shaved head.

AMATO WATCHED BURKE as he paced behind the sofa in the Apostolic offices alarmed by something someone on the other end of his cell was telling him.

"We were briefed but not on specifics," the voice on the other end of the line told Burke.

"So you think this is all he knows?" Burke replied.

"As far as I can tell, Sir."

"Alright. Stay next to Rawlins. If he gets too protective, remove him from the mix." Burke hung up.

The bald white agent hung up his cellphone ending his call to Burke. He was at the end of an alley outside the papal residence just a few yards from the rest of his team.

Aadam was coming out of the building. He was surrounded by Vatican gendarmes and Rawlins signaled his Secret Service agents to seal the perimeter around the alley while Aadam climbed in the armored popemobile that would take him to the G20 summit at the Piazza Navona.

12 VIA DI SAN SEBASTIANELLO. That was the address the Arab man entered into the Alpha and that was the address he was standing in front of. He had left the Alpha two kilometers away and traveled the remaining distance on foot. He was sad to leave the Giulia behind. He left it in good condition, carefully wiping off the interior with ammonia. Especially his fingerprints. He would have liked to be able to drive it out of Rome, but he knew the odds of getting out of Rome, at least in a car, weren't especially in his favor. Duffel bag at his side, he pressed the buzzer on the door to 12 Via Di San Sebastianello.

"Sorry, we are closed for the day" a voice announced on the intercom in perfect Italian.

The Arab man answered in perfect Italian of his own, "Yes, I know. But I have an important package for Signore Roselli."

They buzzed him in. A critical mistake on their part and they would realize it shortly.

The Arab headed inside. The building was leased by a trendy architectural firm. They had built a gothic parapet on its roof and this feature was the reason the Arab had chosen it. As he made his way up the stairs to view it for the first time, he was hoping he wouldn't be disappointed.

A female receptionist smiled as the Arab arrived on the landing in front of her desk.

"Bongiorno," she said with a warm smile.

She was twenty-one, perhaps a little older. It was hard to tell with Italian women in that district. Their make-up was flawless, their complexions unblemished. But not for long. The bullet pierced her forehead and exited the back of her skull. She fell back in her chair, the hole barely noticeable, the blood not yet trickling out.

The Arab man turned towards the other rooms on the floor, his silenced 9mm leading the way.

He was startled by another secretary exiting a copy room. Before she could scream, she suffered the same fate as her colleague. The Arab climbed over the bodies of his victims checking vitals. He pulled out three photographs from his jacket. Two matched the victims laying at his feet. He eyed the third photograph and then turned suddenly hearing a toilet flush.

The door to the restroom opened and the lead architect came out. A well-dressed man in his mid-forties, his face matched the one in the third photograph. His head was down, distracted by the screen of his smartphone. He was a Facebook junkie in the middle of uploading a selfie he had taken earlier in the day. By the time he realized the Arab's 9mm was aiming at his head, the selfie had posted. His final post, as fate would have it. The Arab man chose a chest shot this time. And as the lead architect slumped dead on the floor, the Arab grabbed the man's smartphone and eyed its screen. The selfie was still on it. The lead architect was pursing his lips with a vivacious younger woman in a crowded bar. *How unmanly these selfies were*, the Arab thought. He had never taken one. And today would be no exception.

He crushed the smartphone beneath his boot and quickly checked the other rooms. Empty. He carefully avoided the crimson blood from his victims pooling on the white tile and made his way up the staircase to the parapet on the roof.

Chapter XXII

The papal procession coursed through the throng of onlookers packing the streets outside the Vatican. Rawlins was out in front directing the security detail, his eyes constantly scanning the crowd. Aadam rode in the modified pope-mobile. Bullet proof Lexan shielding him on all sides. Except from the top.

Sol was in the crowd, keeping himself invisible, slipping through bodies like a snake, his eyes jumping back and forth, scanning buildings, faces—anything that could kill the boy he had risked his life to protect. He stayed clear of the gendarmes and anyone else who could identify him as the procession moved onto the Via Del Corso in downtown Rome.

Traffic was cordoned off. CNN and other media stringers were lined up at the barricades feeding commentary to the billion viewers watching the historic event worldwide.

"... The crowd is electrified as Pope Aadam winds his way to the G20 summit where, for the first time in modern history, the Pope will have a seat at the most important economic forum on the planet. Vatican officials have reminded us that this is not unprecedented." a CNN commentator informed. "Throughout most of Christian history the Vatican played an important role in global affairs. It's only during the last two centuries that the Vatican has been sidelined and it looks like Pope Aadam plans to change that."

Inside the White House, the President watched the same CNN commentator on his TV as broadcast footage cut to dignitaries and diplomats assembling in the massive convention hall hosting the G20 summit.

"President McCormick is due to arrive here tomorrow morning," the commentator continued. "Meanwhile, Merrick Grant, former head of JP Morgan and newly elected head of the World Trade Organization will give the opening speech at the Summit. Grant, a close personal friend of President McCormick, is fully endorsed by the President and his cabinet ..."

At a storefront on Via Del Corso, Sol caught a glimpse of the same CNN broadcast on a monitor as footage cut to Merrick Grant, the newly appointed head of the WTO— the President's *close* personal friend, as the CNN commentator put it— and the same gray-haired man that interrogated Sol in his cell with Burke. Sol was shell-shocked for an instant, his mind on over-drive trying to piece it together as he listened to the CNN commentator continue.

"Merrick Grant has an ambitious agenda, in-siders tell us. It's rumored he'll be discussing plans to implement a global economic union along the lines of the U.N.," the commentator reported. "Some analysts say Grant may even float the idea of a single global currency displac-ing the dollar, the euro, the pound and countless other currencies. These plans may find support with Pope Aadam who's keen to throw the Vat-ican's ample reserves behind the world and its poor."

Sol's mind raced. He turned as the papal pro-cession rounded the corner. Aadam was only two hundred yards from him. Sol watched Aadam waving to an adoring crowd. Aadam seemed strangely at ease, like someone who knew his fate. Aadam turned in Sol's direction. The two locked eyes a beat before Sol slipped away, nervous that others would see him.

Sol ducked into an alley scanning the crowd. He eyed an odd-looking beggar, a group of Ethi-opian vendors on the sidewalk, teenagers on their Vespas. The suspect pool was infinite. Sol was on edge. Suddenly, his eyes whipped past the architectural offices at 12 Via Di San Sebastianello, then his eyes darted back to the parapet on its roof—to the glint of metal—to what could be a sniper's rifle poking ever so slightly out the parapet's window.

Sol freaked. He fished one of the two remaining cells he took off the Vatican gendarmes in his pocket. He feverishly dialed a number.

Rawlins was in the middle of the papal procession when he heard his cellphone ring. He answered, hearing a familiar voice.

"Rawlins, it's Turner. The ochre colored building on your left. The parapet—looks like a rifle. Get a team up there now!"

Rawlins spun around. Saw what Sol was amping out about. Rawlins motioned two of his agents towards the parapet, then he rushed to the lead procession vehicle. He barked at the driver through his window.

"Right turn ahead! Turn it now!" Rawlins yelled.

The gendarmes and Italian police reacted herding people out of the way so the procession could turn. Some people in the crowd screamed almost getting run over by the vehicles as they swerved down another street. Aadam watched all this calmly. Calmer than the crowd which started to stampede seeing the change in direction.

Sol watched from down the street dying to get in the act. But he still couldn't trust that Rawlins and the others wouldn't arrest him. So he stayed in the background, hidden by the crowd, keeping watch on Aadam while Rawlins' team cleared the parapet.

Four agents, guns raised, burst through the lobby door of 12 Via Di San Sebastianello. They carefully ascended the stairs to the first floor. They lurched backwards seeing the two dead bodies in a pool of blood on the floor where the assassin left them.

They recovered, cleared the other rooms, then made their way stealthily up the next flight of stairs to the parapet, their guns ready to blow away anything with a heartbeat.

They huddled silently by the parapet's door for an instant before one of them kicked it in. The four agents burst inside.

"Freeze!" the agents screamed in unison.

All their weapons were aimed at a man holding a rifle on the ledge of the parapet. But the sniper didn't respond. He didn't even turn.

"Drop your weapon or we fire!" the lead agent yelled.

The other agents got ready to unload their

clips as—

"Wait!" a second agent screamed.

The second agent moved to the sniper spotting the blood trickling down the sniper's right arm. The agent lifted the sniper's head. The head of a dead man. But not an assassin. It was the lead architect that the Arab man shot exiting the restroom.

The lead agent grabbed his walkie-talkie and yelled a single word to every agent listening—

"DECOY!"

Chapter XXIII

Two blocks away, Sol was tracking the procession, keeping an eye on the parapet. He spotted one of the agents leaning out of its window. Then he spotted Rawlins on his walkie-talkie. Sol grabbed his cellphone and hit redial.

Rawlins answered immediately knowing who it was.

"You get him?" Sol asked urgently.

"Decoy. Our guy left three victims behind and he's still out there!"

"Shit!" Sol yelled as he scanned the buildings around him on edge. He hung up and shoved his way towards the procession feverishly scanning faces. He wasn't worried about being caught anymore. He was just worried about saving Aadam's life.

Suddenly, a Vatican gendarme recognized him. He blew his whistle and signaled two other gendarmes. They closed in on Sol. Aadam spotted the commotion. So did Rawlins. Sol didn't care. He was too busy looking at something he just spotted on a roof a block away—a man with a rifle—the Arab man—Aadam's assassin.

Sol lurched through the crowd towards Aadam. A Vatican agent pointed his gun at Sol screaming—"Stop!"

Sol pointed to the sniper angrily. "On the roof, you idiot!" Sol screamed. "On the roof!"

Rawlins looked upward as Sol jackhammered past the Vatican gendarme and leapt onto the popemobile as Rawlins and everyone else finally spotted the assassin.

"SNIPER ON THE ROOF!" Rawlins screamed into his radio.

The gunman had Aadam in his sights. He squeezed the trigger. The crowd freaked as the shot rang out and Sol jumped through the air— tackling Aadam—knocking him down as the assassin's bullet streaked by the top of Aadam's head.

The crowd panicked. Thousands hit the ground. A few thousand more started running, stampeding their way down alleys away from the chaos and causing more chaos of their own.

The Vatican agents fought to make their way through the melee to Aadam. The youngest Vatican agent had his gun out. Sol trusted no one at this point; he figured the agent might be a backup assassin so Sol raised the .45 he had taken off the guard in the cell. He aimed right at the young Vatican agent's head. The agent backed off. Sol grabbed Aadam forcefully.

"C'mon! C'mon! We have to get clear of here! You're not safe!" Sol yelled as he yanked Aadam out of the popemobile and into the crowd.

The scene was pure chaos. Across the street, Rawlins was racing towards the building where the sniper had taken the shot. Sol used the pandemonium to slip away.

He pulled Aadam into a nearby coffee shop. Seeing this, the locals inside started pointing and yelling—*Il Papa! Il Papa!*

Sol guided Aadam to a back door. He kicked it open and pushed Aadam into an alley behind the coffee shop. Gun raised, he covered the kid, ready to blow away anything and anyone who got close.

He spotted a man getting into his car. Sol knocked him out of the way. The man yelled but was too shocked seeing Aadam and the gun that he didn't resist. Sol shoved Aadam in the car, climbed in the driver's seat and the car sped away.

Two blocks in the distance, the Arab assassin was racing across the rooftops tracking Sol in the car below. He reloaded his rifle, spinning backwards as he heard Rawlins and two other

Secret Service agents racing down the rooftops a hundred yards behind him. Rawlins fired; the assassin dodged the bullet and slipped away.

Rawlins' cellphone rang. He answered and put it to his ear on the run.

"I got the kid. You got the shooter?!" Sol asked urgently on the other end of the call.

"We're on him. Give us Aadam, Turner."

"Can't do that. Not yet. There was a Vatican gendarme who was the backup. There could be more. Can't take the chance."

"I can't protect him if I don't have him, Turner! Now turn him over, dammit!" Rawlins yelled.

"Can't do that, Rawlins. I'm sorry." Sol hung up, flipped the back cover off the cellphone, removed the battery and tossed it out the window as the car sped away.

Sol swerved around a corner. Bad move. He freaked seeing four carabinieri vans coming towards him, sirens blaring. Sol spun the wheel and turned hard right down an alley. He looked over at Aadam who for the first time looked strangely unnerved. Not that anyone wouldn't be, but somehow the boy's inhuman calm had cracked in the chaos.

"I told you. You wouldn't listen. Do you believe me now?!" Sol asked him angrily.

"I believe in God's will," Aadam answered firmly.

"God's not going to save you, Aadam!" Sol yelled frustrated. "*You are not* the Messiah!"

"I never said I was," Aadam replied, finally raising his voice.

"But you went along with it! They programmed you—brainwashed you so they could get you elected!"

Aadam's inner strength was crumbling but he was still defiant—"No! *I know who I am*!"

"So do I," Sol responded, his gut wrenching. "You're the false prophet—the goddamned *Antichrist*!"

Aadam shook his head, nearly somnambulant. He couldn't parse this. As Sol swerved through traffic, Aadam's brain came apart at the seams. The carabinieri vans were right behind them, gaining on them, their sirens blaring loudly, the overpowering noise triggering something inside Aadam—a thousand images manifesting, colliding inside his head—*disjointed fragments of his training—the brain washing. Burke yelling at him in a sterile cell. His body tethered to macabre monitoring devices. Scientists hovering above him. His body writhing on a gurney as they administered electroshock therapy to his skull.*

The horrifying memories overwhelmed him. Aadam started shaking like an epileptic. Sol freaked seeing this as he fought to pilot the car through traffic. But Aadam was in another world fighting hallucinatory madness—an unrelenting stream of tragic images from a childhood lost. But suddenly, in the midst of these, came brilliant flashes of white. Images of a dazzling light from above. An unbearable warmth, a beckoning, a knowing. Aadam's face was frozen in a numb, ethereal calm.

"Aadam?! Aadam, can you hear me?!" Sol yelled, seeing him unresponsive, fearing the boy had gone into shock.

Aadam finally snapped out of it. He turned to Sol incredibly calm and focused until—

BLAAAMMM! The massive roar of metal devouring metal as Sol's car crashed into an oncoming police van. Sol's head impacted the wheel as the vehicles pancaked to a stop.

Carabinieri and Vatican gendarmes poured out of the vans following them as Sol recovered groggily. He forced himself out of the car and made his way around to the other side. Aadam was shaken. Stable, but extremely weak.

"… you are wrong about me. I will prove it to you …" Aadam told Sol frailly.

"Sure. Fine. C'mon!" Sol replied as he pulled

him out of the car seeing the Vatican gendarmes approaching with their guns drawn. Aadam was finally on his feet and Sol tried to pull him away, but it was too late. He was surrounded.

"Release him and don't move!" The Vatican gendarme in charge screamed.

Sol nodded and began slowly lowering his weapon as the gendarmes circled him, closing in when—

The *crack* of a rifle. The gendarme in charge collapsed, a bullet in his head. Sol spun, seeing the Arab assassin down the street, his rifle raised and still firing. *Crack. Crack. Crack.* The gendarmes and carabinieri returned fire as Sol dragged Aadam towards shelter.

Sol spun intuitively towards the assassin. He could feel he was in his sights. His intuition was right. He could feel imminent death as the assassin's finger squeezed the trigger and the bullet left his rifle at 3150 feet per second. It cut through the air at warp speed and ripped into Sol's body as he wrapped himself around Aadam, piercing Sol's shoulder, jackhammering them both to the ground.

Sol groaned in pain as he heard *four more shots*. Sol looked up seeing the bald Secret Service agent firing the four rounds into the assassin. The assassin slumped lifeless to the ground.

He would never be interrogated, he would never drive the Alpha Giulia again, he would never reveal who hired him and most importantly, he would never reveal why.

Sol finally peeled his bleeding body off Aadam. "Are you okay?" he asked the boy.

Sol froze. Aadam wasn't moving. Then he noticed the bleeding hole in Aadam's neck. The sniper's bullet had burrowed through Sol's shoulder into Aadam and severed his jugular. Sol came unglued. He covered Aadam's gushing wound with his hand.

"NOOOO!" Sol cried. "Not letting you die—not like this!"

Sol tried to revive him. Nothing. Aadam didn't move. More Vatican agents raced towards him. Sol's head was spinning. The lead assassin was dead, but there could still be more backups. He couldn't trust anyone. Not now. Not after all this.

Sol grabbed Aadam's body. He dragged it to the car and put Aadam inside. The gendarmes were almost on top of him as he jerked the car into gear and sped away.

Rawlins closed in with his team screaming—"Turner, don't run! There's nowhere you can go!"

Rawlins watched helplessly as Sol's car disappeared around a corner. Sirens blaring, three carabinieri vans whizzed past Rawlins, giving chase. The Vans ran a red light in pursuit. Bad timing. The drivers of the vans jammed their feet on their brakes in unison as a triple-decker tour bus barreled towards them unaware through the green light in the other direction. Two of the vans and the bus collided in an otherworldly roar. The vans went airborne as the bus rolled violently on its side, smashing through the intersection

A block away, Sol eyed the fiery collision in his rear view mirror. He floored the accelerator and sped away from the chaos. He looked over at Aadam keeping his hand pressed on the boy's wound. Aadam had lost a lot of blood but he was starting to regain consciousness. He eyed Sol weakly, compassionately, "... Please stop. ... No need to run," he said.

"I'll get you to a hospital," Sol replied defiantly. "I won't let them have you ... *Can't* let them have you ..."

Aadam was fading but he eyed Sol with tenderness, "So now you finally know ... You were chosen ..."

"What?" Sol replied confused.

Aadam could barely talk, but his words were

necessary for Sol to hear. "Inside you ..." Aadam told him. "All that exists ... All that you need ... Just embrace it ..."

Aadam's eyes closed for a second. Sol shook him. "Stay awake!" Sol commanded. "Don't try and talk, just—"

"Why do you think we were put here?" Aadam interrupted, staring at Sol with a firm lucidity, a final flash of light in his eyes.

Sol, still driving, looked over devastated, watching the kid die.

"I *don't know*," Sol finally answered helplessly.

"... You do ..."

"I *don't!*" Sol replied angrily, wishing desperately that he did.

Aadam's eyes started to tear. "*Yes,* ... you do," Aadam told him tenderly. "Turn inward, listen to the silence ... and *you will find me*."

Aadam smiled softly at Sol as his blood soaked hands clutched the small *leather bound book* he had been writing in over the last few weeks. And then he was gone.

Sol's heart sank. He turned hard down an alley. Skid to a halt. He jumped out. Pulled Aadam onto the sidewalk and draped him across his lap to check his vitals.

But Aadam was dead. The life Sol had been

defending no longer existed. Sol beat his fist on the pavement. He sat rocking Aadam's body back and forth in his arms in denial. For an instant, it was a tragic, gut wrenching image evocative of the Pieta. Sirens blared in the distance as carabinieri scoured the streets of Rome looking for the lost Pope, whose memory would haunt them for eternity.

Chapter XXIV

Small delivery vans brought fresh baked goods to the tiny cafes on Rome's pedestrian walk streets near the Spanish steps. The city was just waking up, its residents unaccustomed to the three carabinieri vans and two black Suburbans roaring down the sleepy calle of the Via Del Croce. They skid to a stop outside of a small pensione called the Hotel Panda.

A nervous receptionist looked up as a horde of Italian police led by Larson and Rawlins barged through the doors to the tiny hotel. She grabbed a ring of keys and greeted the men whom she had obviously called.

"He arrived two nights ago," she told them. "He hasn't made a sound."

Larson nodded and the team followed her up a staircase to the second floor. They wound down a hall towards a door in the back. The receptionist opened the door and the group crowded into a small room in the rear of the hotel.

Larson was the first to reach the body lying

motionless on the floor—Sol's body.

Larson turned him over. Sol's face was pale, his shoulder wound dressed with a torn pillowcase. He'd lost a lot of blood. It pooled around him. Larson checked his vitals. He was still alive.

"Get an ambulance!" Larson screamed at the carabinieri commander.

SOL'S EYES STRUGGLED to focus. Images coalesced into recognizable faces hovering over him in a hospital room in downtown Rome. Michael and Anne were the first he could see clearly. Her eyes were wet with tears. Seeing him finally come to, she smiled with joy and leaned over to hug him. Michael piled on. Sol smiled, tearing up himself. He winced a little, his bandaged shoulder still in pain. Then he eyed Anne confused.

"... I thought they'd taken you. I thought you were lost to me ..."

"They did. But the thugs they sent were pulled over for speeding. Frank had put out an APB on them. Thank God the officer recognized us," Anne told him through her tears.

Sol turned to his son relieved. "How you feeling?"

"A lot better than you," Michael answered

stroking his father's hair, trying to be brave.

"You were always better than me, Champ. That's what kept me going."

The tender moment between them was broken by Larson as he walked in relieved to see his old friend conscious. But he was anxious for answers.

"I hate to interrupt the reunion but—"

Sol nodded resignedly. He knew there were more pressing issues. Like a missing Pope.

MOTORCYCLES ESCORTED THE black Suburban past the Vatican where three hundred thousand people were holding vigil for Aadam. Each held a candle, forming an infinite bed of twinkling white lights.

Inside the Suburban, Sol sat in back alongside Larson. Bandaged and somber, Sol stared at the massive crowd in front of St. Peter's as they passed.

"Do they know?"

"The Vatican hasn't decided how they're going to play it," Larson responded.

"How about *playing* it with the truth?!" Sol replied disgusted.

"It would destroy the Church."

"And what about us?" Sol said defiantly. "*Our* part in it? Who knew? How high did it go?!"

"We don't know," Larson answered feebly.

"The President?"

"He categorically denies it."

"Amato?"

"They've appointed him head of the Church until they find a new Pope."

Sol turned to him furious. "But Amato was in on it! They designed it! A false flag assassination scenario to pin on the Muslims while they produce a new *gospel* to pimp their agenda with Aadam's signature on it! Can't let them get away with it, Frank! We just can't!"

"We're working Burke hard," Larson assured him. "He'll break and finger the principals."

Sol leaned back frustrated, his gut wrenching. He eyed an industrial compound in the distance.

"Turn left here," Sol told the driver.

Chapter XXV

The Suburban turned into the abandoned industrial compound's parking lot. At least one hundred police and gendarmes were waiting for them in squad cars and vans. A limo was parked near the entrance. A man climbed out of it as the Suburban approached. It was Cardinal Amato.

Sol bristled as he looked out the Suburban's window, seeing Amato surrounded by Vatican gendarmes.

The Suburban stopped. Larson helped Sol outside. Amato feigned concern seeing Sol's condition.

"We are all indebted to your courage," Amato told Sol with a saccharin reverence.

Sol ignored Amato and walked past him towards the compound followed by Larson and the carabinieri.

Sol wove his way through the antiquated smelting machinery towards a large rusted metal cylindrical furnace. It looked as if it hadn't been used for decades. Larson studied the furnace's

massive metal door. It was sealed shut and se-
cured by a large brass padlock.

"Why here?" Larson asked Sol confused.

"Didn't want them to have him," Sol answered as he glared at Amato, "I didn't want
them to win."

"Ok. So where's the key?" Larson asked.

"I threw it away," Sol answered calmly.
Then Sol suddenly grabbed the gun out of a hol-
ster worn by a carabiniere. The Vatican gendarmes frantically pulled out their guns thinking
Sol was going to shoot the cardinal.

Sol eyed Amato icily. "Relax, *Eminence*. If
there's a hell I'll be down there with you—so I
can watch you *burn* in it."

With that, Sol turned to the door and shot off
the lock. He handed the gun back to the carabiniere. The Vatican gendarmes holstered their
weapons as Larson's men pried open the door
with crowbars. They all followed Sol inside.

BLINDING HALOGEN FLASHLIGHT
beams crisscrossed the rusted walls of the large
furnace which Sol stopped right in the middle
of—his face frozen in shock.

The beams illuminated the old concrete
floor. *Empty*—except for a pool of dried blood
and Sol's bloodied jacket.

"Where's the body?" Larson asked.

Sol was dumbstruck. "I left him there. Wrapped in my jacket!"

Sol grabbed a flashlight. He waved the beam at every millimeter of the obviously empty furnace. Sol turned to the group shattered. "He was dead. Right there in my jacket! I swear it!"

The others looked at him skeptically as Sol turned to Larson. "How long was I missing?"

"Three days," Larson answered.

"Three …"

Sol's voice trailed off, trying to process it, fathom what it meant. Sol aimed the flashlight at the latch on the door.

"That's exactly how I left it! No one could have possibly gotten in—"

"—Or gotten out," Amato replied equally shattered.

Sol turned to Amato. Each man was overpowered by his thoughts, their brains spinning with the ramifications of this, their worlds turned upside down.

The cardinal dropped to his knees and bowed his head in shame.

After a long, tormented moment, Amato's words ushered forth in a scared, repentant whisper—

"*L'Immacolato …*"

Chapter XXVI

Three hours later, the abandoned compound was packed with more police, two forensic units and a chaotic herd of television crews. One Italian news stringer for CNN stood in front of his station's camera.

"... The body of Pope Aadam is missing," the reporter told his viewers. "The Carabinieri suspect it was removed and taken away by his followers after it was locked inside this compound by a Secret Service agent just three days earlier after Pope Aadam was murdered by a Muslim fanatic. European and American intelligence agencies are hard at work trying to determine the identity of the radical group backing the assassin. Meanwhile, Vatican officials are pleading for the world to remain calm. The Vatican is offering a five million euro *no questions asked* reward for the return of the Pope's body so he can receive a proper burial and a last viewing by the faithful."

As the black Suburban drove out of the gates of the compound, Sol stared out the window as the Italian reporter's camera spun towards him and zoomed in on him for a close-up. Sol looked right into its lens and the shadowy image of him, numb, shattered and confused, was broadcast live to millions of grieving viewers as the Suburban drove away.

THE TIBER RIVER shimmered that night under a full moon. The Suburban drove along the streets above it and Sol watched the river snaking through Rome out his window. The weather was still cold in late March but Sol's window was down. He needed the air, needed to breathe, the colder the better, as if somehow it could bring him to his senses.

But Sol feared nothing would make sense of this. Still, he tried, "Amato's men must've followed me there."

"I'll buy that," Larson answered as he rode in the back of the Suburban alongside Sol. "Hell, you've been right about everything else. Your explanations of the miracles all checked out— except for Jergens."

"I don't understand?" Sol said, finally turning back to him.

"Jergens admitted to Michael's misdiagnosis," Larson replied. "But Jergens swears he never gave him the antidote. Michael *never* got the injection."

"What?!"

"Michael was cured *before* Jergens ever got to him—the day you visited with Aadam."

Sol leaned back, incredulous. His brain on overload, his cynicism under siege. He stared numbly at the Tiber moving past, confused and conflicted, when suddenly--

"Stop the car!" Sol yelled.

The driver slammed on the brakes and the Suburban skidded to a halt. Larson watched confounded as Sol jumped out and rushed down the steep, muddy embankment towards the banks of the Tiber.

AT THE WATER'S edge, Sol stopped and just stood there, his eyes frozen in disbelief. *There*—a hundred yards across from him on the opposite bank—a *naked body* walked near the water's edge. The body of a young man, a body bathed in the moonlight—

The body of Aadam.

Sol stopped breathing as they stared at each other. Aadam's eyes supremely content, Sol's morphing from disbelieving to tearing.

Shaken and nearly somnambulant, Sol struggled to fish something out of his jacket—the small, *leather-bound book* still covered in Aadam's blood.

Sol opened it and eyed the words written by Aadam's own hand. And though the language was foreign to him, he now had the message he was chosen to deliver. The sentinel, the ever-vigilant centurion, finally felt the need to weep.

He looks back at Aadam. A faint smile appears on young boy's lips, then he's gone -- leaving something Sol doesn't see. It's a *plaque*. It reads:

" This is the spirit of the antichrist, which you have heard is coming and even now is already in the world. '

John 1:4

SOL TURNER WILL RETURN IN

THE DARK PROPHET

.

ABOUT THE AUTHOR

Kevin Alyn Elders is an Author, Screenwriter, Producer and Director living in the Pacific North West and Villefranche Sur Mer. From his early works, including the *Iron Eagle* action adventure series, through his later works, including *Echelon Conspiracy*, he has written in many genres. His taut, compelling, suspense-filled narratives have found their latest incarnation in his Screen Novel Series of Paperbacks, Ebooks and Audio Books.

For a list of his Theatrical work:
https://www.imdb.com/name/nm0253106/

ALSO BY THE AUTHOR